Who would be in this maze?

Sissy wasn't naive enough to call out with a "Hello, who's there?" as she'd seen enough horror movies to know that never worked out.

As she began to run, she heard footfalls, faster. She was being stalked. Did her stalker know his way through the labyrinth?

She sprinted down the long hall, walls of hedges so tall and perfectly trimmed blocking her view. But she was being chased. She rounded a turn. *God, let this be right!*

Taking a left this time, she followed it to another choice. *Right.*

As Sissy took the turn, she glanced back to see a man—in black again with a mask—coming for her. She shrieked and sprinted. "Help! Help me! Somebody help me!"

Rounding left, she saw another right. She took it, running fast and long until...no. *No!*

A dead end.

Her breath caught in her lungs. Turning around, she saw no one.

Fear broke out over her body in chills. No way through the hedges. No way over them. It was go back or go nowhere.

And both meant death...

Jessica R. Patch lives in the Mid-South, where she pens inspirational contemporary romance and romantic suspense novels. When she's not hunched over her laptop or going on adventurous trips with willing friends in the name of research, you can find her watching way too much Netflix with her family and collecting recipes for amazing dishes she'll probably never cook. To learn more about Jessica, please visit her at jessicarpatch.com.

Books by Jessica R. Patch

Love Inspired Suspense

Texas Crime Scene Cleaners

Crime Scene Conspiracy
Cold Case Target

Pacific Northwest K-9 Unit

Cold Case Revenge

Quantico Profilers

Texas Cold Case Threat
Cold Case Killer Profile
Texas Smoke Screen

Love Inspired Trade

Her Darkest Secret
A Cry in the Dark

Visit the Author Profile page at LoveInspired.com for more titles.

But I would not have you to be ignorant, brethren,
concerning them which are asleep, that ye
sorrow not, even as others which have no hope.
—*I Thessalonians* 4:13

To Meredith Tipton, your grief coupled with your love and trust in Jesus have been inspiring to me. One day all tears will cease and you will see him again. Until then, you have impacted so many lives and continue to do so by your faith that is anchored in the hope of Christ Jesus.

Acknowledgments

Thank you to my agent, Rachel Kent, and my editor, Shana Asaro, for all your hard work.
And to Susan L. Tuttle and Jodie Bailey.
Brainstorming with y'all is fun. A lot of fun!

ONE

Beau Brighton had finally solved his first case. And not one to sneeze at either. Fender Industries' CFO had been embezzling millions, and Beau had found the money trail earlier today. An arrest had been made, and bringing a jerk like Claude Morrison to justice had felt amazing. Maybe he was cut out for private investigating, even if the Texas media and his father thought it was yet another one of his grand adventures to pacify time.

Let them talk.

He'd helped a company. Been on the good guys' side for once.

That was new—doing something worthwhile.

Only three and a half months ago—the week of Christmas, to be exact—he'd had a serious wake-up call about his life when he'd been suspected of serial murders. One that led him to surrendering his life to the Lord and then going into a partnership in a PI business with his long-time best friend, Rhode Spencer, who'd launched Second Chance Investigations on the side of his day job—aftermath recovery with his brothers.

Beau had always admired the Spencer men, especially Rhode. He'd been a former homicide detective for Cedar Springs, Texas, before going to work for Spencer Aftermath Recovery and Grief Counseling Services. Rhode had hit a rough patch in his life too, but had never given up. Beau admired that most.

Beau had also admired Rhode's twin sister, Sissy. More than he should have. But she didn't do crime scene cleanup. Blood made her squeamish. She'd once fainted when her oldest brother, Stone, punched Beau in the nose and blood sprayed everywhere, including her face.

He'd had it comin'.

But she never held his shortcomings against his sister, Coco. When Coco lost her fiancé in a drowning accident two weeks into the new year, during a winter glamping trip to McKinney Falls State Park, Sissy had been there to help her through the past three months.

His mind wandered as he drove back to their dude ranch in the Texas Hill Country between Cedar Springs and Austin. He'd received word from Rhode that the upcoming birthday party the Brighton family was hosting at their estate was doubling as a wedding proposal from Stone Spencer to his Texas Ranger girlfriend, Emily

O'Connell, the birthday girl herself. They'd gotten together this past Christmas.

The upcoming proposal had put Coco on his mind again. She hadn't been able to get out of bed after her fiancé Kiefer's drowning, but with Sissy's counseling, Coco was now showering and dressing. She had even started to paint again. But the proposal might hit her hard, and Beau wanted to give her a heads-up so she had time to prepare.

The gate to their Texas dude ranch and estate was open, and Reggie wasn't in the guard shack. Odd. Maybe he'd gone into the employees' wing to the restroom. Beau drove past the gate, noticing the contractor and his crew had finally arrived to work on the guest cabins. These days people wanted rustic to be chandeliers and old farm tables. Not cowboy foil packets over an open fire. If the ranch wanted the business, they needed to supply the demand.

Beau followed the wending drive behind the house to the guesthouse. Though it was usually reserved for important friends of their family, Coco had moved out there after Kiefer had died. Beau had tried to convince her that isolating herself wasn't healthy, and that they had their own wings in the main house. She would have privacy. But she wanted seclusion. Randall McDonough, who ran the day-to-day operations on the ranch, saw to it she had what she wanted.

Beau's opinion had been kicked to the curb.

Beau let himself in the front door. "Coke! It's me." He hoped she was in the back room. Randall had made it into a small art studio for her. If she was painting, she was having a good day. Beau hoped to see more and more of those.

While he hadn't lost a fiancée, he had lost the only woman he'd been in love with, and he had no one to blame but himself. He'd done Sissy Spencer nine kinds of wrong when he was eighteen.

Passing through the foyer, he froze.

The house was in shambles. Chairs had been overturned, vases of flowers fallen to the floor—dirt and glass everywhere. A noise dragged his sight to the long hallway, and his heart leaped into his throat. A dark figure was racing away. He started to give chase when another presence came into view.

His blood turned cold.

Coco.

She was slumped in a dining room chair, her head lolled back, exposing her throat and revealing red splotches on her pale skin.

Shoes crunching on broken glass, he raced to her. Making sure she was alive was more important than chasing her attacker at the moment.

He checked her pulse. Nothing. "Coco! Coco, can you hear me?" he asked, her unresponsiveness terrifying him. He fumbled in his pocket for his cell phone. "Siri, call 911." A mountain of emotion lodged in his throat as he began CPR.

Come on. Hurry up.

He checked her pulse again. Still nothing.

Panic broke loose as he continued compressions and prayed he wouldn't fail at this too.

Beau frantically paced the ER waiting area, holding back tears. Coco was the best person. Why would anyone want to hurt her?

After they'd loaded her in the ambulance, he'd given his feeble statement to Cedar Springs homicide detective Dom DeMarco, who was also the Spencer family's cousin.

He should have been able to relay more information. Height and weight of the assailant. Anything. But the figure had been a blur, and once Beau had seen Coco, terror and shock had erased any common sense but to save her. All he remembered was that his security guard hadn't been at his post and the gate had been open. He hadn't registered anything peculiar. The police were checking on Reggie. Right now, he had no news about his guard or his sister.

She might be alive.

She couldn't be dead.

Commotion and voices broke out, and then the Spencer clan barreled into the waiting area. Looked like Dom had called them after he left

Beau. Rhode led the charge, with Stone and Bridge following.

What shocked him most was that behind Bridge was Sissy. He wasn't surprised she'd come to see her friend in critical condition but that she'd come knowing Beau was here. Sissy hadn't been within five feet of him since the summer before she left for college.

The only exception had been the week of Christmas when he'd come by the family ranch, not realizing she'd been there. He'd tried to respect her wishes of space. She'd allowed him to stay and partake of their early Christmas festivities. She knew the Spencers had been more of a family to him than his own. The small mercy had meant a great deal. And there was her wedding...

She cast a quick glance at him, her ebony eyes meeting his under a canopy of long dark lashes. She and Rhode had their mother's Mexican heritage, and it showed in their bronze skin. To him, every other woman fell short. No one was sweet and spicy like Sissy Spencer. When he held her gaze too long, she sandwiched herself between Rhode and Stone.

"I'm so sorry, man," Rhode said as the brothers took turns with sympathies and handshakes. Rhode hugged him. "What did the doc say?"

Beau shook his head. "Haven't heard from him yet. My parents want updates, but my dad's business overrides flying home. Though I suspect Mom will hop a plane as soon as he lets her."

"We need to get a list of anyone who has it out for Coco or anyone who might be obsessed with her," Rhode said and slicked his chin-length black bangs behind his ears. "Didn't you say she felt watched the last couple of months?"

"I chalked it up to the media—they always try to follow a Brighton and even more so since Kiefer's death. I shouldn't have ignored it. I should have beefed up security. Which reminds me. Reggie, our security guard on duty at the time, wasn't at the shack, and I saw a few construction vehicles and vans. We legit have some work being done. But one of them could have been Coco's attacker blending in. I need to talk to Reggie and get the entrance footage. We might have our guy on camera." Pulling his cell phone from his pocket, he called the guard shack. Zeke answered. "Hey, man, have you seen Reggie?"

"No, he wasn't here when I came on duty. He's not answering his cell phone either. There's a swarm of media here and the police, asking me the same questions."

News traveled fast. Too fast. "Don't let any of the media in and cooperate fully with the PD. Call Reggie's wife, see if he's at home. And pull the footage from when he was on duty." A pool of dread formed in his gut.

"Yes, sir."

Beau ended the call and looked at Rhode. "No one can find Reggie. And I fear what we'll discover on the security footage."

"Any word on Coco?" Sissy asked, refraining from making any physical contact with him.

She hadn't laid a single finger on him, not even to hug him at her wedding, but he was okay with that. It would have been too hard to embrace her and then let her go. But he'd been tempted.

Sissy Spencer had been too good for him. He'd tried to keep their friendship platonic. But one night before leaving his house after a swim, she'd kissed him out of the blue. Best kiss he'd ever had. In that moment, he was no failure. The world had belonged to him. And Sissy was the world. They'd kept their relationship a secret. Beau's reputation with girls was never squeaky-clean. But he'd never felt about any other girl the way he'd felt about Sissy Spencer.

Then that one summer night under the stars, he'd ruined everything when they'd been unrestrained. Instead of protecting her and breaking things up before they crossed lines, he'd rushed in with a headiness he didn't want to contain.

Afterward, guilt swooped over him like a tsunami. Dad had been right. He'd had no business getting involved with someone as good and sweet and innocent as Sissy Spencer. He'd failed. Ruined her. His guilt and shame had been overwhelming, and in typical Beau Brighton fashion, he'd ghosted her.

Ignored her calls. Ignored her. Pretended like it hadn't meant anything. Then convinced himself over the years it was better this way—her believing the lie.

"No. No word yet. And quite frankly, I'm scared to ask."

"I know you already told Dom what you witnessed," Rhode said, "but can you tell us while it's still fresh?"

"Truth is, I can't remember much of anything." How would he make a good PI if he couldn't be observant and cool under pressure?

"I understand," Rhode said. "But it's Coke we're talking about. Try to go through it one more time."

Beau nodded and recalled what he could with nothing new surfacing. "Should I have chased him down?"

"No," Stone said. "You made the right call."

He nodded, but didn't feel like he'd done anything right from the moment he walked inside the house.

The doctor entered the waiting area, his face grim as he looked at Beau.

"Is she...?" Beau was too afraid to finish the question.

"A coma. She's on a vent, but she's alive."

Alive. Coco was alive. That precious word

blurred out the rest of the doctor's information. Something about gone too long without oxygen, swelling of the brain, and touch and go.

"She's in ICU. You can go up for a very short time."

Sissy Wells, who was still called Sissy Spencer in these parts, stood in shock at the severity of the doctor's news. Coma. Not enough oxygen to the brain. Possible brain damage. Sissy had been friends with Coco since they were toddlers. Coco had mentioned to her that she'd felt watched at times, but severe loss, like a fiancé's death, could often trigger all sorts of psychiatric disorders.

But who would want to kill her? Had it been random or was it personal? These were the things her brothers and Beau had been discussing before the doctor made his appearance.

Beau looked completely disheveled, his brown-ish-blond hair sticking up everywhere and his piercing blue eyes wide and frightened. Beau loved his sister more than anything. They were as close as Sissy had been with her late older sister, Paisley, who'd died over four years ago. And only a few months before her death, Sissy had lost her father. As a grief counselor, it was her job to help others heal and mend in a healthy way.

But Sissy was a hypocrite.

She was still stuck in the grief and loss. Not only of Paisley and Dad, but the loss of her husband and the baby girl she'd delivered stillborn after the car accident. How could she help her clients and not herself?

"Go on in and see her. Call us if anything changes," Stone said, and he and Bridge left.

Rhode hugged Beau. "We'll find who did this."

Beau nodded. "I won't stop until we do."

Sissy swallowed down her ill feelings and stepped up to Beau. He'd smashed her heart and made it hard to trust others, but he was grieving, and she knew that particular heartache best. "I'm sorry. And I'll be praying that she wakes up with no complications." She reached out to touch him, hesitated, then squeezed his bicep to comfort him. His eyes widened and he glanced at her hand. "If you need anything, I can provide you with a good counselor."

Not her.

"Go on in and see her," she said.

"I don't know if I can."

Sissy understood the fear and dread. The anxiety. "Beau, I know how you're feeling. I've been there. But you can't hide from it."

He held her gaze and she tried not to squirm. She'd always been a sucker for those brilliant blue eyes. When looking at her, they'd been kind and honest and sincere. So she'd thought. Turned out Beau's tongue really was silver, and she'd fallen for his words and let him steal her heart.

"I—I could go with you if you'd like," she

heard herself say. The words shocked her. But she meant them. They were no longer friends, but Beau wasn't faking his fear, his shock or his aloneness. His parents were in France. He had no one.

His eyes filled with moisture and his cheek twitched. "You...you would do that? For me?"

"Coco wouldn't want you to be in this alone." She couldn't lie and say it was for him. It simply wasn't.

He seemed to process her words. Then he nodded once and cleared his throat. "Only one person can go inside anyway. I'll be okay. I'm not alone."

She wasn't sure who might be with him, but she let it go. "Okay, then."

He wiped his eyes. "I do appreciate you coming, though. Thank you. If Coco wakes, I'll tell her you came by to see her, to be here for her."

Sissy's heart broke a tiny bit, and before she thought it through, she hugged him.

At first it was a one-sided hug, but in a few moments, Beau's arms encircled her lightly, then with more strength. She'd forgotten what he smelled like—money and sophistication. And ruggedness. Suddenly, the past flooded back— their friendship, the laughter and late-night talks that turned serious so often. Their fears and hopes and dreams and all the things teenagers talked about during the first months of puppy love.

She broke away and exhaled a shaky breath. "Call us if anything changes."

She left him standing there alone, though he said he wasn't, and she rushed to the elevator, hoping to catch her brother Stone. This was all too much.

Sissy hated hospitals; it brought back memories of laboring in childbirth in vain. Of Todd's death, her father's, her sister's. She met Stone and Bridge in the parking lot.

"Everything okay?" Stone asked as he spotted her.

"No." Nothing was okay. She couldn't stop thinking of the past and how much she'd loved Beau once. She'd had a crush on him since she was nine. Slivers of guilt for thinking of their romance—and not of her and Todd's—pricked her heart. She needed a distraction. "Did Beau say if there was blood at the scene?"

Bridge narrowed his eyes. "No blood. Why?"

She nodded as if it was a done deal. "I need to do something. Coco won't want to come home to a messy house. Beau isn't going to think to ask, and I can't let their house manager do it. She practically raised Coco. So I'm going to go clean up the mess. Has the scene been released?"

"Yes." Stone cocked his head. "But there's no reason you need to do it tonight."

"Coco might wake up. And what if Beau decides to go back there? I don't want him—" She paused, realizing this need to clean the crime scene—to be distracted—was as much for him as it was for Coco and herself. "He doesn't need to see that."

"She's probably not waking or coming home tonight," Bridge said. "You heard the doctor. He won't know much of anything until the swelling on the brain subsides—if it will subside—and it could take days to months. Maybe never."

"Yes, I heard him," she snapped. "But she is going to wake up and I'm going to clean the scene. I have my gear in the car." She raised her chin, daring any of her rough and tough brothers to disagree.

Stone raked his hand through his hair. "I can come help."

"No." He, Bridge and Rhode had been on a long scene today cleaning up after a teenage boy accidentally shot himself. Sissy rarely cleaned the scenes. Blood turned her insides out, but she was always available for grief counseling. The teen's family had turned it down for now. "I need to be alone anyway."

Stone wrapped her in his beefy arms and kissed her head. "I know this is bringing up stuff. Spend some time with the Lord in prayer as you work and don't stay too late."

She nodded and marched toward her car. On the drive to Coco's, nothing but her own tragic life played on repeat. She was stuck in a void of loss, spinning like the farmhouse in *The Wizard of Oz*. She'd yet to be dropped into her new normal where the gray turned to color again and a yellow brick road led her to relationships. She had no ruby slippers to click because home wasn't going to be warm or welcome anymore.

Instead, she continued swirling in a vacuum and faking it until she made it. But she wasn't sure she would make it.

Why did she have to lose so many people she loved? It wasn't fair.

She drove to the gate of the Brighton family ranch, which still had media vans parked outside. She pulled to the gate and met Zeke, the night guard. He recognized her and smiled.

"I'm going to work on the cleanup," she said quietly.

"Yes, ma'am." He let her through the gate, and she drove around to the back where Coco had been living.

She quickly slipped on a hazmat suit, even though there would be no biochemicals. Still, it was easy to clean in. She shivered in the mid-April air. It was cooler tonight than usual. After stepping into special shoes, she pulled on latex gloves, grabbed the cleaning gear from her trunk and headed inside. She'd called her mom and told her that her Cavalier King Charles spaniels, Lady and Louie, needed to stay awhile longer until she could pick them up. Sissy used her Cavaliers as therapy dogs, and Mom, who was undergoing chemo treatments, enjoyed them warming her lap and providing comfort. Her sweet Blenheims could calm the most restless of hearts.

As she entered the living room, she dropped her gear and sighed at the signs of a struggle. *Oh, Coco.* She'd fought valiantly but it hadn't been enough. After placing her AirPods in her ears, Sissy turned on an upbeat Christian station on her Apple Music and got herself organized. She laid out her heavy-duty industrial trash bags, cleaning supplies, rags and extra gloves. She didn't need special waste containers except the plastic one for the glass.

She started on the big items, collecting the broken shards for the plastic bins. Next she righted the couch cushions, put the books on shelves and set the dining chairs back where they belonged.

The biggest disaster came from the coffee table, which had several glass panes shattered. Sissy tried not to think about Coco's fight for her life. Maybe coming here wasn't the best idea after all, but while she swept up glass, she concentrated on the songs about faith in God and remembering that He was always good and faithful.

He had been good to her, but she'd been pretty angry at Him for a while after Todd and their baby girl—Annabelle—had died. For a whole year she'd turned her back on Him, never darkening a church door, cracking open her Bible or listening to a single song of praise.

She wouldn't consider her spoken words, or the words of her heart, kind toward Him. She had learned her lesson with Beau and had made sure she and Todd did things right. They went to church together, prayed together and waited for marriage to be intimate. And still God had taken him and their baby away.

What had she done to deserve such tragedy? Such pain?

Nothing.

Sometimes pain and tragedy happened. Deep down she'd known that, but it was so much easier to blame God for the bad things that happened. He hadn't popped that tire that led to the crash. But He hadn't prevented it either—and that had made her the maddest.

But God wasn't in her pocket to do her bidding. To always see to it that nothing she deemed bad would happen to her. When she came to that conclusion she'd repented.

No longer was she angry at Him. But she also saw no way to move forward without fear that tragedy might strike another loved one or another baby. She was still stuck in the depths of grief that pulled her down like quicksand. No one saw her fighting to claw her way out or to succumb, depending on the day.

That was her invisible burden to bear alone.

She stared at Coco's massive entertainment center. Glass from the coffee table had gone everywhere and that meant under furniture. She slid the broom under the small opening at the bottom of the center and drew out shards of glass, dust bunnies and even a little loose change. Sissy also noticed a black thumb drive.

Tears filled her eyes.

Coco had been working on a memorial album to honor Kiefer. Sissy had encouraged her to comb through photos and begin compiling her favorites in a desktop folder. It was a good way to remember good times, laughs and tender moments.

Sissy hadn't managed to do one for Todd. Some counselor. She'd tried but failed. It was too painful. Too hard. Too much.

Coco had balked at the idea at first for the same reasons Sissy hadn't created one. But then, unlike Sissy, Coco decided to try. It had helped.

She pocketed the thumb drive and swept up the debris with the industrial vacuum, then began cleaning the fingerprinting powder off every piece of furniture, the doors, windows and even the floors. She couldn't say the Cedar Springs CSI didn't give it their due diligence.

When she was finished, she checked the time. It was almost midnight and she was exhausted. Her back hurt, and it was too late to pick up the dogs. They were likely snuggled up with Mama in bed. But she missed them.

Time to lug the cleaning materials and trash outside. At least Coco would come home to a clean house. As if nothing bad had happened.

Except it had.

Sissy started for the front door when the hairs on her neck rose. A cold chill swept up her spine as an awareness of someone's presence prickled her skin. As she turned, a dark figure in a ski mask swung the metal vase she'd replaced on the table and smacked Sissy in the head. Pain blinded her and she shrieked. The attacker dived on top of her, and she bucked and thrashed underneath the weight.

The black-clad figure pulled a gun and put it to Sissy's head. She instantly froze and her breath came in pants.

"Sissy?" a voice called.

Beau! Beau was here.

The attacker froze, then smacked Sissy in the head again, dazing her. He jumped up and bolted toward the back of the house.

Beau entered the living room and spotted the figure, then glanced at her.

"Go! I'm okay," Sissy called, and he blew past her, giving chase.

Sissy's ears rang and her whole body ached. A trickle of blood seeped down her temple. She touched the cut on her head and winced. Trembling, she stood on jelly legs.

Someone had attempted to kill her. She'd had a gun to her head. Bracing herself against the wall, she breathed deep, trying not to pass out from the shock and the two smacks to the head.

It must have been the same person who had tried to kill Coco. Why return? To finish the job? Would he not know that Coco was in the hospital? It had been on the news.

Why attack Sissy?

And would he try again?

TWO

Beau chased the attacker, but in the shadows of night, the jerk got away. Beau kicked himself for not being faster. Had the guy followed Sissy here from the hospital? Why else would Coco's attacker return? Was it the same person who had tried to kill his sister?

Yes. He was sure it was. Two separate attacks on the same night. Both dressed in black. That would be too coincidental. But what brought him back to the house? Sissy?

He rushed back inside. Sissy stood in the living room wringing her hands and breathing deeply. A portion of her jet-black hair was matted to her head with blood. Fear gripped him as he raced to her. "You're hurt." She could have died.

"I'm okay. I checked it out in the bathroom mirror. It looks worse than it is," she said through a quiver in her voice.

Beau glanced around Coco's house. No one would have known that only hours ago, the place had been ransacked and his sister almost killed.

"You…cleaned it up? It's after midnight. How long have you been here?"

"Since I left the hospital. I wanted to…make it better for her…for you," she said weakly.

She wanted to do something nice for him? Sissy had always been thoughtful, but he hadn't expected such a generous gesture.

"Thank you," he murmured. "Coco will thank you too. When she's better."

"I had a feeling you might come back. I didn't want you or her to have to see it this way."

He told her he had returned to check if anything was missing. Find any kind of clue. What he didn't say was that he also wanted to simply be near Coco's things since he couldn't stay in her hospital room in the ICU.

He inventoried the living room. Nothing appeared to be missing. Next he checked her bedroom and studio. After going through the rooms and finding nothing missing, he returned to the living room. "You did this all by yourself?" He still couldn't get over it. This would have been a massive amount of work.

"I didn't mind. Really."

"Did he say anything to you?"

Sissy shook her head. "No. I was cleaning and had my music playing. I never expected anyone to show up. Certainly not a killer. Why return? It makes no sense."

"I don't know. Unless he thought he missed

something, left something behind. You find a weapon or any kind of evidence?"

She shook her head again. "I imagine the CSI team found everything. Wouldn't a killer know that anything he left behind would be found?"

"I'd think so, yes." Beau was confused. "Unless something here is hidden by Coco that can link to her attempted killer. Something the police might not be looking for. Wouldn't seem unusual or misplaced. Or it's hidden so well the killer knew they couldn't find it. And when I interrupted, it kept him from getting it. I'm just guessing, though." Coco didn't keep secrets from Beau. At least, he didn't think she did. Maybe it had nothing to do with Coco and everything to do with something Kiefer had been involved in. Beau had no idea if Kiefer had secrets. Could one of them come back to bite Coco?

He noticed Sissy again. "You're shaking. Let me drive you home or at least follow you. Make sure you get in safely."

Her lips pursed, but then she nodded and accepted. She must be frazzled if she was agreeing to allow him to do anything for her. "I'll let you follow me."

"You sure you can drive? You're pretty shaken up."

"I can do it."

She didn't want to be in the same car as him, more likely. But at least he could see her safely home. He escorted her to her car, then got inside his and called Rhode, filling him in and letting him know he was following her home and would see she was inside and safe before leaving.

Sissy lived about twenty minutes away, which gave him more time to think about who had it out for Coco—or Kiefer. Seemed Sissy might have been collateral damage. He surely hadn't expected to find anyone on the property. He'd check the cameras if the police hadn't already taken the footage.

His father had blamed Beau for the whole thing. As if he could have known any of this would happen. Dad wasn't flying in, and Mom would fly out as soon as she could. When Beau had assured Dad that he'd find out who did this, he'd simply said to let the real police do their jobs. Dad did not support Beau in this new venture. But then, Dad had never supported Beau in anything.

Beau had been a failure since coming in second place in a coloring contest in first grade. He'd been so happy and excited. Dad had told him second place was just first-place loser. Brightons didn't lose.

That had been the first of many of Dad's pep talks to Beau. Beau learned quickly it was easier to not start or to give up than to finish and fail. He shook off the grisly memories and pulled up behind Sissy. "Can I come inside?" he asked, stepping out of the car and meeting her at her driver's-side door.

"No. I'm fine." She turned to start up the walkway and paused, looking back. "Thank you for showing up when you did. And following me home." Her words softened as she spoke and moisture filled her eyes. "I have no idea what would have happened if you—" She choked on her words and Beau reached for her, but she flinched. His heart pinched.

"Are you sure I can't walk you inside and stay awhile?"

"No. I just want to go to bed." She trudged up the walkway to the porch, unlocked her door and entered. When he saw a lamplight glow, he waited a few beats, then got inside his car.

What was the attacker looking for? And why couldn't they find Reggie? Was he in on it or was he an innocent bystander who might have been in the crosshairs?

He realized he hadn't gone through Coco's safe. He was going to comb everything again meticulously. Whatever the attacker was after, Beau was going to find it first.

Sissy laid her purse on the coffee table and shivered as the earlier events replayed in her head. She would love company and comfort right now, but not from Beau. While she was grateful for his intervening and felt sorry for his situation, he was still Beau Brighton—the man who'd used her and wrecked her. She didn't blame him for their passion or for getting carried away. She made all her own choices. But she'd let herself believe that she wasn't a shiny object he wanted to chase. She wasn't another conquest or pastime until something better came along.

Turned out she was all those things. And that devastated her for a long time.

Until she met Todd. And even then, he'd had to work slowly to build her trust.

She wished she had him here in their little cottage three miles from the family ranch. A place they wanted to fix up and raise a small family in until they could afford to build a bigger place and a bigger family.

Now it was spacious enough for just her and the two dogs. A heaviness settled over her like a looming shadow, weighing her down. She wanted the dogs' companionship tonight, but it was far too late to wake her mom. It was nearing 1:00 a.m. and her adrenaline still raced. Until it crashed, she was wide-awake. She decided to make a cup of herbal tea. While the kettle heated, she pulled her hair into a sloppy knot on her head and took out her contacts.

The kettle whistled and she poured the boiling water over a peppermint tea bag into her mug. She missed her dogs prancing into the kitchen as if they expected a spot of tea themselves—it was in their English nature, and they wanted Mommy to give them a sip, which she never did.

Mommy. The word was bittersweet. She loved her fur babies, but nothing had filled—or never would—the loss of Annabelle Marisol, her middle name after Sissy's mother. The smell of peppermint permeated the house. She added sugar and headed for the couch, where she curled up with her grandmother's quilt. It was tattered and worn—like Sissy.

She switched on the TV music channel for light background noise in the dark, quiet house. Instrumental strings and guitars played as she sipped her tea and tried to wrap her brain around the earlier events. She had sent a group text to her brothers and her soon-to-be sister-in-law that she was unharmed and fine. It wasn't a lie but it was a stretch.

She opened up her laptop to scroll through piling work emails. That might tire her out. When she wasn't working for the grief counseling service, she worked part-time for a dog training facility, helping pets become therapy dogs. She shifted on the couch and winced as something dug into her thigh.

Coco's thumb drive.

She'd forgotten she had it. She'd meant to put it in Coco's art studio after cleaning up the glass. Fishing it from her pocket, she decided she could use some good things to put into her mind, and seeing Coco's photos of Kiefer and her progress would do the trick.

She pushed it into the USB port and watched a folder appear on the desktop.

Kiefer Sterling and Coco Brighton

When had she changed the name to that? It used to be *In loving memory of Kiefer J. Sterling*.

She clicked on the folder, opening it. Inside were dozens of photos and a video. Had Coco compiled a memorial video out of old footage?

Sissy clicked on the first photo and shifted on the couch. A spray of photos filled the screen in glossy black-and-white. None she'd seen before. These appeared to be professional quality.

An eerie sensation squeezed her gut. She clicked and the next photo slid into view.

Coco and Kiefer in the woods on their glamping trip with friends the weekend he died. They were sitting around a fire.

Next was Kiefer during an early morning hike. Sissy checked the time stamp on the photo. The day Kiefer died. But Coco couldn't have taken this. She'd been asleep. That was part of the guilt she'd unnecessarily felt—not having been there when he'd accidentally fallen and hit his head on a rock. The fall had rendered Kiefer unconscious and he'd drowned in the lapping waters of the bank.

Confused, she clicked through several more

photos of him hiking that day and photos of him resting while he sipped from a thermos.

What on earth was going on? Who had taken these and why? Why were they on Coco's thumb drive? Had someone sent them to her? Had someone been hired to spy on Kiefer? Sissy's mind swirled with confusion and the need to find answers.

It didn't feel right.

Someone was stalking him in the woods with a camera. Could it have been the same person Coco had felt watching her?

She clicked another photo and a strangled cry erupted as her hand flew to her mouth.

Not Kiefer.

This photo was a close-up of Coco going into the funeral home for Kiefer's service, with tears streaking her cheeks, her face a blotchy mess. Several more photos revealed Coco in different places—at the graveside after the funeral, leaving a rose on the casket, crying on Beau's shoulder and staying behind after everyone else began leaving. In each picture, the crowd was blurred out.

The photographer's focus was directed on Coco alone. Close-ups as she grieved.

What was going on?

This obviously wasn't Coco's thumb drive. It belonged to her attacker. Which meant he must have brought a laptop—unless he'd used Coco's and swiped it when he left, but Beau hadn't mentioned that. The thumb drive might have fallen when he grabbed it and ran. Sissy wasn't sure how else it would have gotten underneath the entertainment center unless during a struggle.

A new thought struck her and stole her breath. That was what the attacker must've returned to Coco's for. He must have taken the laptop, which would have had the photos on them. No time to erase them when Beau interrupted him. He'd grabbed the laptop, dropped his thumb drive and come back with hopes of finding it.

But why take the photos in the first place? What would be the motive?

Sissy dared one more click and another set of photos popped up on the screen.

Coco in her living room having therapy sessions—with Sissy. Someone had lurked outside, hidden, and used a telephoto lens to invade Coco's world—her sorrow. Not just one session but many had been captured by the camera.

But there were even more.

Coco going into a support group meeting in Austin. Coco visiting Kiefer's grave alone three weeks ago. It had been her last trip to the grave site. She'd decided it wasn't productive for her mental health right now. She'd resolved to visit on holidays and his birthday. She had to begin to try to move forward. Baby steps. That had been her first baby step. Then painting again. Which she'd taken up two weeks ago, and Sissy had noticed a little light come back into her eyes.

Coco had also joined a Bible study at the church especially for women who had lost a family member. The friendships she'd been building with like-minded believers who had gone through loss had been a great source of encouragement.

But this…this was a violation on so many levels—from stalking her personal life to trespassing on her grief. There were no photos of her painting, reading a book, going to the grocery store. Just of her most vulnerable moments—of pain, loss and grief.

It was sick.

And confusing.

Sissy finally reached the video. Should she press Play? What would appear on the screen? She feared seeing something she'd never be able to unsee. But she had to know.

Had to watch.

With trembling fingers, she slowly pressed the play button on the first video.

The videographer appeared to be wearing a camera like a GoPro. She watched as a chill rippled down her spine and hairs rose on her neck. The instrumental music playing on the TV no longer sounded soothing but ominous and foreboding.

She muted it, unable to listen any longer but not wanting to turn it off and be plunged into complete darkness sans the laptop light. Sissy's heart lurched into her throat and her stomach roiled.

The videographer held a bloodied rock in a gloved hand as an unconscious Kiefer lay motionless by the water's edge, red running down his cheek.

Tears sprang to her eyes and she clutched her chest, the ache inside excruciating as she watched in horror while this person dragged Kiefer into the water, face down.

Kiefer hadn't fallen and hit his head, accidentally drowning.

Now the videographer spoke, voice modulated to sound like the villain in that horror movie Sissy had watched back in college.

"Coco," he said, "here is the truth. He didn't die tragically. While you slept and dreamed of a future, growing old with Kiefer, I hit him with a rock and I'm drowning him in the lake. I thought you'd like to know something else. You're about to die too."

The video went dark.

Silence filled the house except for Sissy's sobs. This was the sickest thing she'd ever witnessed. Horrifying. Mortifying. The killer had been planning this all along. He'd known when he killed Kiefer he was going to kill Coco too. Was she the real target? Or had he targeted both of them?

The police had to have this thumb drive. Now.

A floor joist squeaked, freezing her in place. Breathing hitched, she listened through her pulse pounding in her ears. She now wished she'd taken Beau up on his offer to come in and stay awhile.

Maybe she'd imagined the creak.

Regardless, she needed her cell phone, which was on the charger near the front door. As she stood, a shadowed figure emerged from the hallway.

She opened her mouth but nothing came out. Not a single shriek or scream. Fear knocked every thought from her brain and her body shook so violently she thought she might be having a seizure. The intruder came for her and fight-or-flight kicked in; she bolted for the phone and the front door, but she wasn't fast enough.

The phone clattered on the hardwood and she fell with a thud, the attacker's weight on her back.

"I didn't want it to be this way." The voice was raspy and unfamiliar—maybe modulated.

The hands were strong around her neck. She reached out for the dogs' tug rope and clutched it. Flinging it over her head, she struck the side of the attacker's head, the hard knot the dogs loved to chew pelting it with force and giving her a window of opportunity to inhale air and scramble away.

Snatching a glass vase off the entryway table, she chucked it, then threw open the front door with shaking hands as headlights blinded her.

She lurched forward, half jumping, half falling from the porch steps, and stumbled, not sure if she was running to friend or foe.

Beau's pulse spiked as Sissy ran from her house and nearly fell off the porch steps. He grabbed his gun and jumped out of his car as she raced toward him.

"He's in there! He's found me!" she screamed, stumbling her way into his arms.

"Get in the car and lock the doors. Drive away if you need to." Beau bolted into the house, then slowed, reminding himself to be cautious and stay against the walls as Rhode had trained him. Beau switched on the overhead lights, illuminating the empty house. Room by room, he cleared it until he was secure in the fact that the intruder had fled. He locked the door leading from the kitchen and made his way to the front porch. His sigh was one of relief when he saw Sissy in the driver's seat of his idling Audi RS e-tron GT, her hands white-knuckling the steering wheel.

He jogged to her and she opened the door. "Is he gone?"

"Yeah, he's gone. Are you hurt?" He noticed the red splotches on her neck. Fury rose in icy waves.

"Just my throat and my elbow hurts, but I'm alive," she replied. "Barely. If you hadn't shown up…again…"

He helped her from the car, debating whether to embrace her, but deciding against it based on her earlier reaction. Instead, he escorted her inside, noticing her slight hesitation upon entering.

"It's clear," he said, holding her unsteady gaze. "I promise. It's safe." Restraint was killing him when he desperately wanted to reach out and touch her cheek, give her comfort.

She blinked then swallowed and cast her eyes on his car. "Why are you here this time of night... or...at all?" Curiosity mixed with confusion in her tone.

The question of all questions. Why was he here?

He'd gone back to Coco's and searched it, finding nothing. Then he'd returned to the main house. It was drafty and lonely, and he'd turned around, climbed into his car and driven aimlessly.

Here.

A safe place. He wasn't sure what he was going to do once he turned off the car. Maybe just sit and think. Keep watch. The Spencers had always felt like family, and at one time Sissy had been much more to him. His secret keeper. Confidante. Truth teller.

Well, it didn't matter anymore.

"I guess I wanted to double-check on you and I'm glad I did." He noticed her laptop open and a cup of tea on the coffee table. He'd never been here before. This was Sissy and Todd's place.

He'd only met the man a few times around the holidays.

And at the wedding reception.

That had been miserable to watch. Coco had shown him the family invitation. Not that Sissy had specifically included him—his lack of invite was unspoken. But she hadn't specified, and he couldn't resist going to see her in a bride's gown.

He wished he hadn't.

Looking for Rhode, he'd wandered the quiet church hall only to see her step into the hallway alone. She'd knocked the very breath from him. No one could hold a candle to Sissy Spencer.

"What are you doing here?" she'd asked with a hint of irritation and a fair amount of shock.

I love you. Please don't marry him. Those words sat on the tip of his tongue. Instead, he said, "I got the invitation."

"Oh. Why are you back here?"

"I was looking for Rhode." Not completely true. Maybe deep down he had been looking for her. Looking for a way back to her. To undo all the wrongs and make it right. To tell her that all the times he talked of forever he'd meant it.

But he'd been afraid and a coward.

"He's in the pastor's office with the other groomsmen and Todd."

Beau had taken a few steps toward her, searched her eyes and had caught a dose of fear in them. He had messed them up. Ruined any good thing between them, and she'd been happy with a man who loved and adored her. A good man. Better than Beau had been back then. Maybe a better man than Beau was now.

In that moment, he'd swallowed down the words. Vowed to get over her and not mess up the one special and sacred moment she deserved. "You look beautiful. I wish you…" His voice had cracked. "I wish you the very best, Sissy. All the happiness and joy that life can bring you. Truly."

One single tear bloomed in her right eye. He'd never forget it. He'd wanted to wipe it away. "Thank you," she'd finally murmured.

He'd left her in the hallway, taken the back-row seat and felt the joy of her happiness and the pain of his aloneness.

Now he surveyed their home. It was all Sissy. Soft coastal colors, warm browns and some antique pieces proving her to be a sentimental woman. The whole house would fit into his garage designated for the twelve vehicles he'd accumulated over the years. Twelve cars revealing he'd been chasing after elusive happiness.

He ought to sell them. Most of them.

This little house felt more like a home than his estate. Recently, he'd been thinking about leaving. No reason to stay. Not when — He halted the thought and forced himself to leave old memories in the past where they belonged. Instead, he focused on her attack. "Can you tell me what happened? Was he here when you arrived?"

"I don't think so. I don't know. He came from the hallway."

"Your bedroom window was cracked open."

Sissy pinched the bridge of her nose. "I guess I forgot to lock them. I like to keep them open during the day when it's nice spring weather, and it has been."

Beau didn't reprimand her. It would be easy to forget. "I wish I knew why he set his sights on you. Is it because you got away at the house? I don't understand." It didn't make any sense.

"I think I know why he was there and why he came here." She cocked her head and tears filled her eyes. "I don't know how long he was there watching me. But he must have caught me." Her lip quivered.

"Caught you how?"

"When I was cleaning, I found something under the entertainment center. I assumed it was Coco's project on her thumb drive. I put it in my pocket and finished cleaning and forgot about it. Until I got home."

"But it wasn't Coco's?"

She shook her head and wiped her eyes. "I think he came back hoping he could find it, that it escaped the police's notice and the CSI. Which it did. It was under there good. Nothing was out of place on the entertainment center and the authorities would have had no reason to be looking for it, I suppose."

"But you interrupted him."

"Yes. I think he was coming here to try and see if I had it. Maybe swipe it and go. I don't know." She ran a trembling hand through her long black hair. "I thought it was the memorial to Kiefer she'd been working on. I had no idea. He saw me watching it."

"Watching it?" Beau frowned. "Watching what?"

Sissy's inhalation was shaky. "I have to show you something, but it's going to be shocking and very difficult for you." She perched on the couch and scooted her laptop closer.

He sat beside her.

"I'm sorry you have to see this."

"It's okay," he murmured. "I'll be okay." But he wasn't so sure.

"Wait." She ran her finger over the empty USB port, then clicked on a folder on the desktop titled *Kiefer Sterling and Coco Brighton*. She frowned. "It's gone. He took it." A sense of realization dawned in her dark eyes. "That's definitely why he came. To get it back. And now he knows for sure I've seen it... I know the truth."

"What was on that thumb drive, Sissy? What is the truth?"

She began to describe the photos and goose

bumps rose on his arms, and then she told him there had been a video.

"Of what?" he dared ask as he sat stunned and numb at the same time.

Sissy clasped his hand, a sure sign that things were about to get worse. "Kiefer was murdered. The video was proof." She recounted the video and the horrific words to Coco at the end in the modulated voice.

What kind of monster would do that to Kiefer, to his sister? The time it would take to stalk, photograph and film… It was mind-boggling. It would take precision and patience. And why?

One thing was clear.

This sicko knew Sissy had seen the thumb drive. She could prove that Kiefer's death wasn't a tragic accident but a homicide.

"Sissy, you can't be here alone. I can stay or I can take you up to your family ranch, but I fear…" He didn't want to terrify her, but she had to know she wasn't safe anymore.

"I know," she said with a shaky voice. "I'm collateral damage. I've seen the truth."

Grabbing her hand, he shifted and gazed at her. "I won't let him hurt you. No matter what."

She held eye contact, then slowly extricated her hand from his and stood. "Beau, I appreciate your concern and I believe it's genuine. But I have brothers who can take care of me."

Sissy might as well have laid him on railroad

tracks and sent a train speeding over him. Unfortunately, she only had his past to measure him by and he'd failed. Never followed through with anything, including her.

"Why are you choosing this profession anyway? Haven't you been groomed to run the family oil empire?" she asked.

Groomed was a loose term. He attended meetings and went where Dad told him to go, but he typically passed the duties off to someone else. He'd been called lazy for that. But those people didn't know his father like Beau did. And Sissy knew good and well he never wanted the family business. But he hadn't balked at the money.

"The way I've lived put me at the top of a suspect list when someone killed five women this past Christmas, and if Stone and Emily hadn't caught the actual murderer, I might be sitting in jail. After that nightmare, I wanted to do something rewarding and meaningful. Like Rhode. Like Stone and Bridge." He hesitated. "Like you," he whispered. "Rhode is the only one who has consistently believed in me. You know I never wanted to run the family business."

"Honestly, Beau, I can't be sure you meant anything you said."

His heart felt the punch. "That's fair. And you may not believe this either, but I am going nowhere. I'm not backing down or quitting."

Her mouth slid south and her eyes said it all.

She didn't believe a word coming out of his mouth. Beau had a lot to prove. To himself. His family. And to Sissy.

"I'll find who killed Kiefer and attacked Coco, and I'll protect you to the bitter end." He would. He'd do whatever it took. He'd pay any cost. He owed her that much at least. "My word's not good or I'd give it. I guess I'll just have to prove it." Deep down a niggle of doubt tried to spring free. Beau hadn't followed through with anything before. But he was a new man now—a man of faith.

His cell phone rang. Zeke. For normal people it would be a ridiculous hour to call, but Zeke was on the night shift. He answered. "Hey, Zeke. You find Reggie or hear from his wife?"

"Yeah, boss." His tone sounded grim. "I got the footage you asked for too. The cops took it earlier but I made a copy first. I'd have sent it earlier in my shift, but the media has been like an owl swooping down on a mouse."

"I understand. It's fine. I could have seen it at the station, though. You didn't need to make a copy."

"I don't trust no cops, Mr. Brighton. Sorry. Not after all that went down at Christmas with the governor and all those crooked officials covering up crimes."

Understood. "What about Reggie? Is he okay?"

"I think Reggie might be dead. Check the footage I emailed you."

Beau's head pounded. "Okay, thanks." He ended the call and checked his email from his phone. As he did, he explained the situation to Sissy, then clicked on the video.

"Can I watch too?" she asked.

He held out his phone and she had to sidle up beside him to see the small screen. Her shoulder brushed his bicep, and he caught her sweet cotton-candy scent.

According to time stamps, twenty minutes before Beau arrived a white van stopped at the guard shack. The driver was hard to make out with a ball cap pulled low and dark sunglasses. The logbook was signed—a fake name no doubt. Reggie let him in.

After driving through the open gate, he got out of the van. Below six feet. Slender. Maybe a runner. He motioned to Reggie, who left the guard shack, then climbed in the van behind the driver. Six minutes later, the driver clambered out alone and drove into the main circle drive behind construction crews, blending in. Beau had seen the van when he arrived.

Nothing indicated the man had been harmed, but the camera didn't record inside the van. Anything could have transpired.

The attacker had fled Coco's and driven right out the main entrance. Beau's blood boiled. He could have caught him.

But Coco might have died if he hadn't gone to her aid.

"Why would he abduct Reggie?" Sissy asked.

Beau blew out a frustrated breath. "My best guess is he knew he might have to flee fast without having to stop and wait on the gate. So he lured Reggie inside with a lie like needing help with something heavy. Once he was back there, he either incapacitated him or he killed him. No one has found him or the van yet...so I fear the worst."

"Why not take the footage from the guard shack?" Sissy asked.

"He didn't have time. I walked in on him, and he had no idea what would happen next or who I might call. I imagine had I not shown up, he'd have stolen it if he could."

"What do you think he'll do now?" Sissy asked.

Beau couldn't be sure.

But there wasn't a single scenario that didn't involve Sissy dead.

THREE

"I think you're being stupid," Rhode said, and Sissy snarled.

"Well, you *are* stupid."

He threw his head back with a dramatic eye roll. "Really? That's what you're coming back with? A six-year-old's response?"

It was the best she could do. Her twin brother was aggravating her to no end. Last night, after Beau had been like the old Beau who had stolen her heart, and offered to stay the night with her, she'd balked big-time and called Rhode. He'd called Bridge and Stone and within minutes the entire house had been filled with testosterone. All three of her brothers had bunked in her house, but she'd told Beau to go on home.

There had been a slight pause and a twinge of hurt in his eyes, but she didn't want Beau here. It brought back the eighteen-year-old Sissy who had given herself to him, knowing it was wrong on every level. But in a moment of weakness and desperate love for him, she'd abandoned her beliefs. Only to be humiliated the next day by the very same boy who had pledged his love and loyalty to her alone. To know she'd been a long con, a challenge accomplished, still nauseated her. And people said Beau Brighton never followed through. Well, he had with Sissy. Followed through with writing her off like the others. A nobody. A conquest.

She'd been overwhelmed with pain. Not only for the way he'd responded, but for ignoring her convictions. Mama always said that sin cost a person more than they wanted to pay and took them farther than they wanted to go. Those words were true. Sissy had made her peace with God and never crossed that line again. But being near Beau was a stark reminder of her past, and the shame and guilt were rearing their ugly heads. He wasn't only a reminder of his inflicted pain upon her, but of her own.

"Sissy," Rhode said, "you should stay home. Or come to the ranch."

Sissy collected her purse. "I love you. I love all y'all. Really. But when a killer came after Emily, no one forced her to not work."

"Finding killers is her job," Rhode said. "She's a Texas Ranger."

"Well, I'm not trying to find a killer, Rhode. I'm just trying to do *my* job. People are grieving. They need me. Need the dogs. And I have dog training to do so others can help even more people. You think the attacker is gonna show up at a dog training facility or Ms. Landoon's and kill me? We have German shepherds and Dobermans trained to protect. I feel safer there than I do here with you and all my brothers!"

Rhode raised an eyebrow. "Now, *that's* a grown-up insult." He clutched his chest and stumbled backward as if he'd been hit by a bullet. Then he straightened. "Fine. But Beau is going with you."

"Oh, no, he's not." That did set her off. "You can go if you think it's necessary, but I don't want to be around him."

Rhode sighed. "Sissy, make your peace with Beau. He dumped you a million years ago. You married another dude. Unless there's something I don't know about…"

She wasn't about to discuss her indiscretions with him. Not about this. They were close and always had been. But some things were private. She stood her ground.

"I have a case. And you know Stone and Bridge are in Austin working a crime scene since six this morning."

A family had gotten into an argument and one of the brothers had shot the other brother. Didn't kill him but it would be ugly. Stone hadn't even offered Sissy's services. "Working helps me."

"It's called *evading*, but I won't lecture you." Rhode rubbed the back of his neck. "Beau is trained. He's actually a great shot—and that's just from being a Texan. And you know he's done boxing and karate and all that jazz since he's been a kid."

"Never got his black belt. He quit boxing for kickboxing. Quit that for the next thing and rinse and repeat. I can't believe you trained him and then invited him into the business." Given Beau's track record, he'd leave and Rhode would end up doing this job alone.

"What's the name of that business?" He eyed her hard.

Second Chance Investigations. "Touché—ish." Did Beau Brighton deserve a second chance? He'd never apologized. Not really. It was as if ignoring what he'd done would make it go away. He'd never explained why he'd used her like that and been so cruel as to completely disregard her. "I don't trust him."

"I do. You know I'd be in a gutter somewhere if I hadn't been given a second chance and even third, fourth or fifth."

Whatever. She didn't need a lecture from Rhode. But it was true. He'd been in a big-time mess with his drinking, and the family hadn't abandoned him but rallied.

And Beau had rallied for him too. She had a sneaky suspicion he'd pulled strings to get him into the best rehab facility in Texas and footed the bill too. Sissy never asked, but the Spencers didn't have the kind of money it took to get him into that place. Not even if Stone and Bridge had spent every penny they owned.

"I'm going to Ms. Landoon's, then the training facility. I'll be home later." She grabbed her phone and shared her location with Rhode. "I sent you access to my every move. If it makes you feel better."

"It doesn't. But thanks. Hey," he said with his signature smirk, "you gonna hunt for that old broad's treasure while you're there?"

When they'd been kids, rumors had circulated that the once-famous actress had hidden a huge treasure somewhere on her Texas estate. She was a little eccentric, and a recluse now, but she was a sweet woman with all kinds of fun stories of her days in Hollywood starting in the fifties, including her brief romance with James Dean before he died. Mostly she was lonely and loved the company of Lady and Louie.

"No. And you better not give it another go either. Just stay off the property altogether. You and Bridge." That moron had actually scuba dived as a teenager in the massive lake behind her house thinking he'd find something buried underwater.

He hadn't.

"Be careful," Rhode called.

Sissy left and stopped off at the family ranch and picked up her sweet Cavaliers. Mama was happy to have them. She even had a little color on her cheeks this morning. After visiting for a few minutes, Sissy put the dogs in their car-seat harnesses and headed the twenty-two miles to Lorna Landoon's estate at the edge of Cedar Springs.

She wasn't going to let some would-be killer keep her from helping others, even if she was fearful. Hiding wasn't an option. However, stupidity wasn't one either, so she would stay alert of her surroundings and keep an eye on the rearview in case someone tailed her. And she had made sure to have her mace and folding stick that could crack a skull securely in her purse.

Instead of listening to the radio on her drive over, she spent it in prayer. Finally, she turned down the long-paved drive to Ms. Landoon's estate, in awe, as always, of the manicured lawn that went for miles. No neighbors in sight.

She drove up to the massive home, only slightly smaller than the Brighton ranch, and parked behind an older-model red car that belonged to Ms. Landoon's newish caretaker. Sissy couldn't remember her name, but she lived in the main house. Sissy hadn't actually met her since she normally came on Fridays, when the majority of the staff had the day off.

Sissy approached the front door and knocked, the dogs sitting like perfect little pooches awaiting their workday. The door opened and a woman around Sissy's age, maybe a bit younger, stood before her in a pair of worn jeans and a thin sweatshirt. Her blond hair was piled on her head and her facial features were pretty but frazzled. "Can I help you?" she asked.

"I'm Sissy Spencer. I meet with Ms. Landoon on Friday mornings."

The woman spotted the dogs. "Oh, the dog lady. Of course. Sorry."

The dog lady. That was a new one, at least to her face.

"I'm Teegan Albright. The Jackie-of-all-trades round here. I'm normally off on Fridays, but I guess you know that. Anyway, Ms. Landoon's been a little restless this week and asked me to work today." Her blue eyes—like perfect spheres—with long lashes gave her an innocent look, and her lips were the kind women paid big money to have. But it was clear hers were au naturel.

"That's sweet of you," she said as she entered the house. "You like working for Ms. Landoon?"

"Oh, yes. She's been good to me and the babies."

"Babies?" A twinge of heartache hit her ribs.

"I have twins."

"I'm a twin!"

"Me too," she said enthusiastically. "Identical? I'm identical."

"No. I have a brother. But I always wished it had been a twin sister." She wouldn't trade Rhode for the world, but he could be super annoying at times growing up—and now. And Paisley had been almost five years older than her, so by the time Sissy needed good boy talk, Paisley was off at college.

Teegan's grin faltered and her brow pinched as if Sissy's words reminded her of something she couldn't quite recall. Then she shook her head and smiled again. "They're almost two, and to say they're a handful is an understatement." She laughed but Sissy heard the exhaustion in her voice. She longed to know that kind of joyful exhaustion herself. "They're with a friend today, though Ms. Landoon loves having them around. She says it keeps her young and reminds her of her twins when they were that age—she had fraternal twins too."

"Lot of twinning going on."

Teegan laughed. "Right? Personally, I think watching me chase them all over creation and go out of my mind is what's most entertaining to her. She's kind of a sadist."

Sissy cackled, really taking a shine to Teegan. She followed her into the massive sitting room filled with Victorian furniture—no knockoffs here. The grand stone fireplace had been lit. Sissy didn't mind; the mansion was drafty and Ms. Landoon was ninety-one. Still, the woman was sharp and spry for her advanced years.

Ms. Landoon sat in her burgundy wingback chair, a pair of one-pound weights resting on the side table. She wore her thick white hair in an elegant chin bob that framed features that had once rivaled Ava Gardner, right down to the lovely green eyes. She was tall and lean and wore a lavender tracksuit.

"Well, I was beginning to wonder if you were going to show today." She spoke with the mid-Atlantic accent Hollywood stars had perfected in the golden age. So upper-crust and fancy. So fake.

Sissy was literally two minutes late and that was due to chatting with Teegan.

"Ms. Landoon, lay off," Teegan said. "She was talking with me. Did you know Sissy's a twin too?"

"I know everything, doll."

"Then why did I have to explain what an emoji was to you?" Teegan teased. Sissy liked their interaction. Teegan was clearly good for Ms. Landoon.

"And call me Lorna—the both of you." She spotted the dogs and grinned. "Come, little ones. I have treats." The dogs obeyed and climbed into her lap.

"I'll bring some tea and leave you two to chat. If you need anything you can text me. Another thing she didn't know how to do until me. Now I'm so blessed that she does. Blessed all the live-long day." She winked at Lorna and zipped out of the sitting room to make tea.

"I like her."

"She's spunky, Sissy. I like spunk. I like her kids too. The boy's gonna give her fits. Mine did. Still does." Lorna rarely talked about her children. They weren't exactly the Brady Bunch. "But let's not talk about me. Let's talk about you. You do not look well, doll."

"I'm not here to dump my issues, Ms. Landoon. You don't pay me for that."

"Sissy Spencer, if you haven't looked up my net worth, you should. Except it's inaccurate. It's far greater. Your fees are chump change."

"Maybe I should have charged more," she teased.

Lorna smirked. "You should have. But I chose you because you didn't. You were fair. And I appreciate that. Now…what ails you?"

Sissy wasn't sure where to start. Teegan returned with tea, then quietly left them. Sissy poured the tea into bone china cups, added cream and sugar, then handed a cup and saucer to Lorna before sipping on her own delicious, proper tea. "Coco Brighton was almost murdered."

"I read about that in the news. You're friends?"

"For a long time." She shared the truth and went so far as to tell her about Beau. Everything. It all tumbled out and felt so good to share. She'd kept it bottled up for ages.

Lorna had finished her cup long before Sissy was done with the story. "That is absolutely dreadful. I worry about you." She placed the cup on the saucer with a soft clink. "I'd be happy to pay to get you a bodyguard. They're usually attractive too. I wonder if that's some kind of job requirement."

Sissy snorted. Lorna was kind, but she didn't need a handsome bodyguard. "My brothers are on it."

"And Beau—he's handsome like your brothers. A requirement, just like I said. I knew men like Beau. Loved men like him. Did I tell you about my fling with Paul Newman?"

Sissy's mouth dropped open. "No, you did not."

"It was before his second marriage. Short. But lovely. I should write a tell-all book. Or maybe I already have." She winked.

Was that the buried treasure on her property? Bridge would be sickened to know all that diving was for the dirt on Lorna's life before she came to know Christ.

Lorna laughed. "I've lost men like Mr. Brighton. Broken hearts of men like him—they do have hearts, you know. Though it takes a special woman to burrow into it. But once you do, you have a lot of influence. Maybe now that you're both mature adults, ask him. You deserve the truth."

To hear him speak the words would only make it worse. But she had all but let him off the hook with no confrontation. Maybe Lorna was right. "I wasn't the special woman who burrowed into his heart. Worked out the best in the end. I loved Todd completely. Still do."

"Sometimes people do hurtful things to others and the reasons are not for spite. Hidden reasons that have nothing to do with the person they hurt but everything to do with themselves. Ask. You might be surprised. Or not. But you'll at least know." She grinned. "You ask and get an answer, I'll reward you with my Paul Newman story. And if you do it within the month, I'll throw a Dean Martin romance in too."

Sissy feigned shock, then laughed. Talking with Lorna had certainly relieved some of her stress. And the older woman had uncannily read her unspoken desire. She had wanted answers from Beau all these years.

Maybe it was time to ask.

Maybe not.

"I don't know. I'll consider it," she told Lorna. "Things haven't been the same since Todd died. I guess I'm just missing him and lonely."

Lorna reached over and laid a bony hand on hers, the diamonds in her rings twinkling. "Do you know what makes me feel better when I'm down, doll?"

Sissy was almost afraid to ask. "What's that?"

"A walk in the labyrinth."

Sissy had never been in the huge labyrinth on the back of the property. The boys had, though. But not by invitation. "Why do you have that out there?"

"I was at a crossroads when I moved here. I'd left Hollywood and that life behind. I had the maze created to remind me that we all have a path to take. Sometimes it feels like a dead end. But it's never really. We just have to turn around and retrace our steps until we find a new direction to take. Eventually, it leads to a satisfying life. Though at times, it's frustrating—double backing and thinking you know where you're going only to get stopped short."

Life was very much like that.

"Once you find your way out, there's a garden that is glorious. And you smile and forget you were in that place for so long!" She laughed. "I believe that's what it will be like when our life here is done. When we meet our Maker. We'll forget all the pain from the hardships, turnarounds, dead ends, from repeating the same path knowing it's going to end at a roadblock. No, we'll not think about that when we see the paradise on the other side." She fiddled with one of her rings. "I learned this the hard way. But God was gracious and He never gave up on me. He's been my companion for many years now."

No more sorrow. No more tears or pain. Sissy

longed for that day. But she was still living here. In the labyrinth of life. Facing what felt like a dead end most of the time. Unsure of where she took a wrong turn or if she'd ever looked at God like a companion who was always with her. "Maybe I shall go for that walk, darling." She giggled at her own mimicking of Lorna's accent.

"You could have been a real doll in Hollywood. I'm glad you never will, though. Fame and fortune don't nearly as often bring happiness as much as they bring pain and emptiness."

Sissy would never know. She had neither fame nor fortune and, quite frankly, didn't desire either. She'd seen what it had done to Beau—and even Coco. She loved her friend dearly but she often could be snooty. Sissy had always helped bring her into reality.

"Let the dogs stay. I have more cookies in my pocket for them. And if you want the secret to the maze—rights are better to take than lefts." She winked.

"If only life were that easy. Stay right." She supposed in a way staying right with God would eventually lead to the garden. Maybe Lorna had it done that way on purpose.

"Have fun, doll. Think it out. Pray it out."

Sissy left the house and wandered to the back lawn where the labyrinth began. It was large and daunting. Over nine feet tall. She could not see a garden beyond it. Had no idea one was even there. But that was the point.

No risk, no reward.

She entered the maze, popped in her right Air-Pod only and pressed Play on her go-to playlist when she was down in the dumps. Worshipful songs about God's faithfulness, His kindness and His mercy and grace. She followed the maze until it came to her first crossroad.

Keep right.

It lengthened and she admired the pots of flowers that had been strategically placed, though she didn't envy the gardeners who had to walk this thing to keep them watered and looking vibrant and fresh. A large bench rested near several pots of early spring daffodils. She didn't much feel like sitting but she stopped to enjoy the flowers, a foreshadowing of the glorious garden to come.

At the next crossroad, she paused but chose to go right again.

A noise, like the hedges being brushed, put her on alert. She froze, listening. Then she let out a long sigh. Who would be in this maze? But as she took a step, she heard rustling. Maybe the gardeners watering the flowers?

She wasn't dumb enough to call out with a "Hello, who's there?" as she'd seen enough horror movies to know that never worked out. She turned right and hurried, no longer enjoying the maze.

She wanted out. But the sound came from behind, which meant she couldn't go back that way.

Forward was her only choice.

What if she hit a dead end? Then what? Panic sent a frenzy through her blood and she bulleted forward. As she began to run, she heard footfalls, coming faster. She was being stalked. Did her stalker know his way through the labyrinth?

She sprinted down the long hall, walls of hedges so tall and perfectly trimmed blocking her view. She rounded a turn and had the choice to cut right or keep going straight.

She chose right. *God, let this be right!* Grabbing her phone from her pocket, she scrolled, fumbled and kept running as she dialed 911.

No signal! Seriously?

Taking a left this time, she followed it to another choice. Left now or right up ahead.

Right.

She ran up ahead, and as she took the turn, she glanced back to see a man, in black again with a mask, coming for her. She shrieked and took off like a rocket. "Help! Help me! Somebody help me!"

Rounding left, she saw another right. She took it, running fast and long until… No!

A dead end.

Her breath caught in her lungs. Turning around, she saw no one. Had he missed a turn? Fear broke out over her body in chills. There was no way through the hedges. No way over them. It was go back or go nowhere.

Either choice meant death.

God, please help me.

When no assailant appeared, she figured he must have taken a different turn.

She crept back the way she came, staying close to the wall of hedges, kicking herself for leaving her purse inside with her mace and defense stick. She worked to make her ragged breaths quieter as she inched toward the turn to double back.

What if he knew she'd hit a dead end? That she'd have to return this way?

He could be lying in wait. But she had no choice. Next to her was another pot of daffodils sitting on a clay plate. Easing down, she hefted the pot off the holder and set it down. Then she used the heavy plate as a weapon.

Sissy would not go down without a fight.

She turned into the next section, gripping the makeshift weapon, and awareness hit.

The attacker dived onto her. The plate hit the ground, shattering.

Picking up a shard and hoisting it like a knife, she swiped at him. He howled in pain as his hand instantly went to his torn shirt and bloody wound beneath. She struck again, screaming. Thrashing him off her, she scrambled to her feet and ran, gripping the shard so tight it drew blood. The sticky red sight nauseated her. But she trudged ahead.

She would not die in this maze.

Shrieks from behind the house sent chills up Beau's spine and his feet into action; he raced across Ms. Landoon's yard. Rhode had called him to keep watch on Sissy with a warning to be prepared for a fight. She'd made it clear she didn't want protection from anyone, especially Beau.

Now he was inside the labyrinth, making his way through the hedges. Fear had his pulse racing faster, and he gripped his gun tighter.

A bloodcurdling cry echoed through the air and tightened a vise around his heart.

He dodged left then right, racing down one stupid tunnel to the next like a blind rat in a maze.

"Sissy! I'm right here, heading for you."

He hit a dead end and growled, then turned around and raced back the other way, taking a right turn over the left. He followed the zigzags, awaiting a new crossroads and hoping Sissy would be alive when he reached her.

Why had she been out here to begin with? She'd seen a million thriller movies with him. Had none of them taught her a lesson?

One didn't get inside a rat race alone when a killer was on the prowl.

It was easier to be irritated than terrified. Because he could not imagine not making it to her in time. He could not bear to look on a lifeless body. Seeing Coco had been gut-wrenching enough.

Sounds of footsteps came toward him, and he aimed, waiting for them to come into view. Sissy rounded the corner, eyes wide and blood streaking her forearm. She clutched a terra-cotta pottery shard in her hand. She shrieked again, startled, and he lowered his weapon, quickly drawing her behind him for protection. "Is he following you?" he whispered.

"I don't think so. I stabbed him. He's wounded."

Beau had never been happier to see her. Alive. Clever and quick thinking to transform a piece of pottery into a shank. He could kiss her, but instead, he maneuvered her into the bend of the boxwood hedges. "Stay here. I'm going to check it out. Please don't go anywhere. I may not be able to find you…but he could."

She nodded emphatically and he ignored sound reason. He framed her cheek, red from running and fear. "It'll be okay. You're safe now."

Sissy didn't shove his hand away. In fact, it felt like she leaned into it. But it was so brief he wasn't sure if it happened or was only his wishful thinking. Beau slunk around the corner and kept to the sides of the boxwoods, moving slowly and listening for any movement.

He wove and wended his way through until he discovered dots of blood sprinkling the paved walkway. He followed the blood until he reached the end of the maze, which opened into a gorgeous English garden; he'd seen many on his trips to England with his family.

There was no sign of the assailant and he lost track of the blood in the dark grass. Turning, he raced back inside, remembering his way, and found Sissy squatting in a ball near the hedge where he'd left her.

"Sissy," he said, and she raised her head off her hands that had been snaked around her bent knees. Tears stained her cheeks and her lip quivered. Beau dropped to the ground beside her and pulled her against his chest, embracing her and rubbing her arms. "It's okay now. He's gone. You got him pretty good, too. It's okay."

Rocking her against him, he laid his cheek on the crown of her head, listening to silent tears become muted sobs. Beau's gut clenched. How could he make her better? Make her feel safe? How was he going to stop this killer who wanted to end her life for what she'd seen on that thumb drive? How would he bring justice to his sister's attacker—maybe killer if she didn't make it?

The doctors had said earlier that there was no change, and they were waiting on the brain swelling to go down. His parents hadn't flown out yet, but Mom had called him before seven this morning to inquire about Coco, to get Beau's side of the story and any updates on finding the monster who did this. He'd wished he had more to tell her.

Sissy's arm wrapped around his waist and startled him. Her grip on his shirt shocked him even more. "I'm so scared. I'm just so scared."

He kissed her head and stroked her hair. "I know. I promise it's going to be okay." Beau hoped his words weren't spoken in vain.

Suddenly, she stiffened, and then her head popped up as she released her hold on him. She jumped to her feet, fully aware she'd been wrapped up in him in the moment. He felt the guarded wall go up between them again. But for a few moments it had been like old times, before he'd let it all go to pot and driven a wedge between them they'd never be able to dig through.

Sissy wiped her eyes, smoothed her hair and sniffed. "We should get back to the house. Check on Lorna and Teegan."

He wasn't sure who Teegan was but he nodded and stood, brushing his hands on the sides of his jeans. "Sure."

"Why are you here anyway?" she asked. Same question as last night.

"Rhode called. Need I say more?"

She grimaced. "No. But I'm once again in your debt," she said reluctantly.

"I'm not keeping score, Sissy."

"No?" she asked as she walked ahead of him. "I find that hard to believe. How many of us are now notches on your belt? Or bedpost, I should say."

Well, that was low-down. But fair.

He didn't answer right away, unsure of what to say and feeling the weight of his shame. Finally, he said, "You were never a notch on anything. Never a score."

She paused, then continued forward, keeping several steps ahead of him until they reached the opening of the maze. "I'll be driving myself home. Don't follow me. I'll call Rhode or one of my brothers, or even Brad."

"Who's Brad?" he asked, feeling a pang of jealousy under the grief her words caused, the grief his actions had precipitated.

"He owns the dog training facility. Or I can call Abe. He's skilled in jujitsu. He's the senior dog trainer and we're friends."

"We should see about your cut." He ignored her very obvious shots at not wanting him to help her, but he'd been the one to save her bacon from the three attacks.

"I'm fine. I held on to the pottery shard too tight and cut my hand. It looks worse than it is. I don't need stitches." At the front of the house, she stopped at the porch and rang the bell.

A young blonde opened the door and looked at Beau first. "Hey, I recognize you."

Join the club.

Sissy turned and caught his eye. He knew that female expression well. Too well. She was checking to see if he was checking out Miss Blondie with the blue eyes. The only woman on this porch he'd even want to attempt to check out hated him. So much she'd rather die than have him protect her. That was saying a lot.

Sissy huffed. "Beau, Teegan. Teegan, Beau. Are y'all okay?"

"Yeah, why?"

Sissy told her what transpired in the maze.

Teegan gaped, then caught sight of her hand. "Come in and we'll clean that. You poor thing." She glanced up at Beau. "Come in. Please. Not taking no for an answer."

Sissy rolled her eyes, but Teegan's invitation wasn't one of flirtation or interest. He knew those tells well too. She was concerned, and she'd been startled to see him on her doorstep. That was all. Once upon a time that might have flattered him. Now? He couldn't care less about being known. He'd love a little obscurity.

After Sissy's wound was cleaned and bandaged, the house secure and the dogs ready to go, he followed her outside. "Sure I can't be of—"

"I will be fine all by myself." She stomped to the car and loaded up the dogs while he slowly made his way to his vehicle, studying her the whole way. She was putting on a real brave front.

Suddenly she growled and kicked the tire of her car.

It was flat as a pancake. Sticking out of the tire was a very big, very sharp knife.

FOUR

After calling the police, Beau leaned against his car, waiting to see if Sissy would ask for help or shoo him off the Landoon property. Instead, she opened her hatch and lifted the flooring, then rolled out a spare. It bounced on the ground and landed in a thud. Next she dug out the jack and wrench for removing the lug nuts.

This woman was ridiculously awesome. Tough. Resourceful. And he had to admit witnessing a woman fully capable and confident in changing her own tire was pretty hot. But it was only flat because a knife was sticking out of it, and while he waited patiently, inside he was a wreck. What if Rhode hadn't called him? What if he'd been ten minutes late? The thoughts sent a new rush of panic over him. He would do his very best to protect her, but how good was his very best? Was it enough to fulfill his vow to keep her alive and unharmed? She'd already been harmed since he'd made that promise.

Did she even realize he was still here, standing by watching and waiting to help? Clearly, she didn't need it. She worked quickly to remove the lug nuts, not once griping about dirt in her nails. The women he'd dated were more concerned about their appearances and how good they looked on his arm. The only mud they'd be interested in was the kind that cost a lot of money to soak in at a spa.

Sissy had always been independent and fearless. But she was afraid now. She'd admitted it, and he suspected changing the tire was her way of fighting back—of trying to gain control of her fear.

"I know you're standing there," she said as she diligently worked. "Guess this will be evidence." She nodded at the knife stuck in the tire.

He dared not ask if he could take it from here and finish the job. She might knock his head with a tire iron. Blue lights flashed as the Cedar Springs PD patrol cars and a white van barreled up the drive. "Maybe we'll get prints from the knife or DNA from the blood in the maze that will lead us to the perpetrator."

Sissy snorted and began tightening the lug nuts, one at a time. "*Perpetrator.* You sound like Dick Tracy." She glanced up as the officers headed her way.

"Ma'am, you need any help?" It was her cousin Dom DeMarco, who worked as a detective for Cedar Springs PD. Now he was the only detective since the former had been on the take in the case her brother Stone and his soon-to-be fiancée, Emily O'Connell, had worked this past December.

"Har har." Dom's failed humorous attempt to pretend she was a stranger wasn't funny.

Dom's Mexican features were similar to her and Rhode's—their moms were sisters, if he remembered right. He sobered. "For real, though, you okay?"

"Yeah." She glared at Beau. "I'm good now."

Dom followed her gaze. Beau caught the hint of disdain in his eyes. Cops didn't always love private investigators. Fair enough. "Gonna need a statement, Brighton."

Beau nodded and gave him his account; then Sissy gave hers. The CSI team had already headed for the labyrinth in search of DNA and to collect other trace evidence. Sissy wiped her hands on a rag in her car and her dogs poked their heads out the back seat's open window. She had those cute fur balls trained better than some children.

"I've been thinking about what we found on the footage," Beau said. "My night guard sent over a copy. It appears our killer—"

An SUV pulled into the driveway. Rhode's blue Honda Pilot. He stepped out, a scowl leading the way. "What did I tell you?" His attention was lasered on his sister. "Better yet, what did you call me? Stupid. Inept in a roundabout way. And you nearly got yourself killed. So you get to deal with me, then Bridge, and we'll save Stone for last."

Sissy's frown slid from her face and was replaced by dread. "How was I supposed to know a killer would find me here?"

"It's called anticipating that he's everywhere." He huffed, then hugged her. "You hurt?"

"Not really." She returned the embrace. "Scared. He flattened my tire. I changed it. Beau watched."

Throw me under the bus like a loser, why don't you? Beau kept his voice calm. "Would you have let me change it for you?"

"No."

"Exactly. And had I asked, would you have given me an earful? Yes," he answered for her. "It's called *anticipating*. Therefore, I didn't ask or offer."

She shoved Rhode away and rolled her eyes at Beau. He ignored her less-than-grateful attitude. She was mad at him and it was a coping mechanism—not one he liked, but he wasn't going to call her out on it. He had his own way of coping that was equally toxic—pretending he didn't care about anything or anyone.

Rhode had her repeat what happened. Then he listened to Beau's account. "We need to tighten up security."

"Agreed." Beau nodded. "I'm not sure why he's doing this—killing Kiefer, then stalking Coco before trying to kill her." Just the sick thought sent a shudder through him. "I think we need to see if we can find other MOs like this. Accidental deaths for the man—specifically fiancé or husband—then the murder of the woman later on, probably strangled. If he's been at this, it's likely we'll find other victims that fit this pattern. But we still need to see if anyone had it out for Kiefer. Run both trails."

Rhode grinned. "You have a knack for this." Then he turned to Dom. "Stretch out several counties too. Maybe this is an isolated incident given Coco is high-profile. But it's smart to look and see. If anything does pop, it'll help us track this nasty guy. He's clearly smart. The way he's waiting so long in between killing the two partners. If that pattern isn't established, then he wouldn't be on local PD radars. Bridge has FBI contacts. I'll have him look into Kiefer. If he has anything hiding in his closet, Bridge'll find it."

Dom inhaled deeply and exhaled slow. "I'll run other accident-murders through the system. See what I see. We haven't found the white van or Reggie yet, but we're still looking. Any news on your sister?"

Beau shook his head. "Just waiting on the brain swelling to go down for further testing. I went by there before I came here. She doesn't look like herself." It was hard to see. "I'll go back later. Sit with her."

"I'd like to go by," Sissy said, "but I have a feeling that no one is leaving me alone anytime soon."

"You want us to?" Rhode asked. "Leave you alone?"

"No. I mean, yes. I don't like having someone with me every moment of every day, but I know this is serious. I'm not naive or stupid—"

"I beg to differ," Rhode said. "But good. I'm working a really nasty divorce case, so I have to be in Austin in an hour. Beau, from here on out, you're lead, but I'll be checking in and take over at night, or get Bridge or Stone."

Sissy's lips pursed. "Why can't you give Beau the divorce case?"

"Because."

Her eyebrow rose but Rhode ignored her. "Give Coco my love," he said. "They say coma patients can hear."

The front door opened and Teegan stepped out. Rhode's dark eyebrows inched north, and he cast Beau a wily smirk as he mumbled, "Yes, indeed." After another glance, he turned for his Pilot. "See y'all later." As he reached the vehicle, he shot the caretaker one more look. Beau wasn't surprised. Rhode always was a sucker for blondes. Though he'd figured Rhode would stick around to meet her.

Teegan watched, frowning, as Rhode's SUV circled the drive and zoomed down the road.

"Sorry to be taking up homestead on the property," Sissy said, drawing the woman's attention from Rhode's car. "Is Lorna doing okay?"

"Yeah," she said in a distracted voice. "She's fine. She loves melodrama, but I wanted to check on everyone. Anyone need a water or anything?"

"That's mighty sweet of you, Miss..." Dom said.

"Albright. Teegan Albright."

"Ha. You and Beau share some of the same last name," Dom noted.

Sissy bristled.

Beau took a step back. "We're actually about to leave. CSI might be here a little longer, though. If you need anything at all, Detective DeMarco can give you a business card."

He noticed Sissy's eyes widen as she realized he wasn't interested in the pretty blonde. Wasn't using Sissy's case as a chance to make a move on a woman. Though her cousin didn't seem to mind. Dom stepped in, handed Teegan his business card and struck up a chat about safety. Beau turned to Sissy. "I'll follow you to the shop for a new tire. Then we can figure out what's next before going to the hospital."

Sissy's espresso eyes softened. "Sounds good."

They said their goodbyes, leaving Dom and Teegan talking.

After dropping off the car, they headed for Cedar Springs General. At the hospital, Beau escorted Sissy inside with the dogs. She thought Coco might know they were there bringing her comfort. "Dom seemed to take a liking to the caretaker."

"Yeah, well, so did Rhode. And Rhode always gets the girl," Sissy said through a snicker. "If he wants her, Dom won't have a fightin' chance." She stole a peep at him. "What about you? You gonna jump in the pretty girl pool, make it a competition?"

Beau felt the blow, though she hadn't dealt it maliciously. Often, he, Rhode and Dom had played games. Mostly when they were much younger. "I don't do that anymore, Sissy. Neither does Rhode, for that matter. We aren't twenty anymore."

Sissy remained quiet and Beau decided to clue her in a little further.

"I gave my life to the Lord three months ago. I'm working through consequences of my past behavior, but I'm trying to live my life in a new way. I'm not interested in vying for her affections. I'm not interested in *her* at all."

Sissy paused at the elevator and scrutinized him. "I didn't know that. Rhode didn't tell me."

"It's private, and I guess public too, since I'm not hiding it. Anyway, my life is going to look different now. After what happened at Christmastime, I realized I needed a change. Rhode had made a change, and if I'm being honest, you've always been an inspiration in the way you lived your life for God. So…there ya have it."

Sissy studied him again, searching his eyes to see if he was revealing the truth or running a con of some kind. She had no reason to trust him. But he saw it then. She did believe him. "That's wonderful, Beau. I always prayed you'd come to know Jesus in a personal way."

"Now you can pray I catch this guy. And maybe we can pray together for Coco."

She swallowed hard and blinked several times. Had he said something wrong? She didn't answer, just gave an almost unperceivable nod and stepped inside. They took the elevator up to the ICU in silence.

"Go on in. I'll be out here," Beau said. "Give you some time with her. I saw her earlier and I'll be back later."

She hurried to the hall, and he thought he saw her wiping away tears. Surely, they were over Coco and not something Beau had done or said. Sissy Spencer had cried enough tears over him. He didn't want to be the source of any more. He sat at a table in the waiting room, sipping a cup of coffee and feeling awful for the others inside the room. Three women huddled in a corner, silently crying. An elderly man paced the floor with his cane, concern evident in his scrunched features.

Another woman quietly read the Bible as she rested in a recliner. Beau remembered what his pastor had shared with him from scripture. That the God of all comfort would comfort him in his suffering. He needed comfort now. And peace. He also prayed for it for the others occupying the same space as they waited on news about their loved ones.

He'd felt peace after giving his life to God, and he knew his sins had been forgiven, but he hadn't quite been able to forgive himself or ask for Sissy's forgiveness for fear she'd deny him.

After about an hour, she returned to the waiting room with red-rimmed eyes. "I hate seeing her this way," Sissy said. "I put the dogs on the bed for a minute and they just laid their little heads in her lap. I told her they were there." She choked on the words and wiped her eyes.

"I'm sure she felt it."

Sissy sighed. "Beau, I'm sorry for being so snarky and ungrateful. You've saved me three times now, and you have so much to think about and deal with. I haven't once thought about that. I've been selfish. But I'll do better."

Emotion clogged his throat. She wasn't selfish. Never had been. "I understand and I appreciate it. Let's get something to eat after we drop off the dogs. We both need a bite."

She nodded. "Okay," she said with no hint of irritation that they'd been together like glue for a while. Because that was exactly how he was sticking to her from now on. Like glue.

They dropped the dogs off, Sissy putting them in their spacious kennel full of bedding, toys and water. She gave them each a treat, and then they headed for a little Mexican joint that made the best tamales in green sauce.

Sissy ate Beau's weight in chips and salsa as she gave him her weekly schedule. Work. Training dogs at the facility, more work. Seemed that was all she did. After eating a delicious meal that left Beau wanting a nap, they headed back to Sissy's.

As they turned on her road, Beau saw the smoke and flickers of light.

Sissy sat straight up. "Beau?" she said, concern hitching her voice.

He punched the gas, rounded the corner and slammed on the brakes, his heart in his throat.

"My dogs!" Sissy jumped out of the car and raced toward the engulfed house. The front porch and front of the house was a raging inferno.

"Sissy! No! Wait!" He called 911 as he raced after her.

But she'd bolted inside.

Sissy's heart slammed into her chest as she entered the burning house. Her precious dogs were inside. They must be terrified. She wasn't about to acknowledge that they might have perished.

As she raced into the kitchen, smoke filled the house and hovered like a cloud of darkness, heavy and blinding. The heat was almost unbearable. She coughed, her lungs itchy and burning.

She had to get to the living room, where the built-in kennels had been placed. Dropping on her hands and knees, she covered her mouth and nose with her shirt and began crawling through the kitchen. Popping and groaning from above terrified her. She'd all but crawled into a bonfire, but her fur babies needed saving.

Coughing, she flattened onto her belly and army-crawled. Fire licked the east side of the house and overhead. Debris fell in sheets, a piece of wooden beam landing only a foot beside her. She shrieked but forged ahead, praying God would keep her dogs safe and well.

Eyes burning and lungs tight, she glanced up to see a flash. She rolled to the side as another section of the wooden beam crashed beside her feet. Finally, she reached the kennels. She wanted to soothe the Cavs, but her throat was raw and she couldn't speak. Coughing, she unlocked the kennel only to find it empty.

No! Where were they? Lady and Louie couldn't have escaped. So, where were they? Fear consumed her like the fire around her. It had now reached to the west side of the house, and a new hysteria played havoc with her brain. How had it eaten its way across the house this fast? Could she get out the way she came in?

She tried but the front door was engulfed in flames and the temperature was growing from unbearable to frighteningly unmanageable. Black dots formed before her eyes; her muscles were relaxing, too relaxed.

Tired. So tired.

She coughed, her lungs burning even more. Where were her babies?

Her thoughts became disjointed and she became disoriented and groggy. Where was she?

Hands grasped her. "Todd? Oh, Todd," she breathed and wrapped her arms around his neck. "I've missed you so much." She kissed his lips and nestled her nose into his neck, pressing gentle kisses to him, savoring his strength and the coolness of his skin. "I can't believe you're here. Where are we? Where's Annabelle?" She hacked as he lifted her into his arms.

He was taking her away.

They'd be together.

No more pain. No more longing. No chasm of grief holding them apart. She clung to him but something didn't feel right.

She returned to his lips, pressing hers against his, showering him with affection, attempting to intensify it, to reveal how much she'd missed him and longed to be near him.

But he wouldn't engage.

Wouldn't kiss her back.

Wouldn't let her longing take flight.

Lacing her hands into his hair, she tugged his head toward her. "Kiss me. Please kiss me."

"Sissy, stop, darlin'," he tenderly whispered. "Just…please just rest. You're safe."

Rest. Yes, rest. She was so tired. Tired physically. Emotionally. Mentally. Tired of trying to hide her grief. Tired of keeping up like everything was normal. Nothing was normal. Never would be again. She was tired of pretending to move forward and onward. "I am tired, Todd."

"It's okay. Lay your head on my shoulder and rest. I got you. I've *got* you," he said, and she heard the break in his voice.

"I'm so lonely," she cried into his shoulder. "I miss our baby."

He cradled her head against him and tightened his protective grip on her…and rest came. A blanket of safety enveloped her, and for the first time in a very long time, she didn't feel alone. She felt loved and cared for.

And yet it still didn't feel right. Todd didn't smell like himself. Didn't touch her like he normally did, and he'd never called her *darlin'* before.

But someone had. Deep in the recesses of her mind, it rolled forward, inching along, almost connecting.

Then blackness swept over her thoughts.

When she awoke, she wore a hospital gown and lay in a hospital bed. While she could breathe easier, her head pounded and her thoughts remained fuzzy as she tried to piece together why she was here.

She raised herself up and caught a motion from the chair on the other side of her bed.

Beau.

His face was filthy and his clothes and hair matched. He had a white bandage wrapped around his wrist and part of his left forearm. "Sissy. How you feelin'?" he asked, gentleness laced with concern.

"I don't know yet," she said through a hoarse throat.

He handed her a foam cup of water with a straw and she sipped, relishing the coolness on her desert-hot and dry throat. "You scared me, Sissy."

"What happened?" Confusion clouded her memories.

"Your house was on fire, and you ran inside to save the dogs." He scooted closer to the bed.

The house. Fire. Lady and Louie. She shot straight up. "Where are they?"

"I went back in but I couldn't find them. The firefighters put out the fire and searched, but there's no… The dogs weren't in the house. But the fire department did find the point of origin. The fire was set maliciously. On purpose."

Tears gathered in the corners of her eyes. Someone had set her home on fire and her dogs were missing. "I don't know if that's good or not. If they aren't there, where are they? Who has them? What was done to them?" An excruciating ache surged through her bones. "Why would anyone take them?"

"I don't know, but we'll find them." Beau clasped her hand and she let him, a memory surfacing at the feel of his touch, but she couldn't quite bring it to the surface.

She touched her lips. "How long have I been here?"

"About two hours. Your brothers are in Austin and didn't want your mom to know. She's not feeling well today. I told them you're going to be fine. Just needed to monitor your oxygen levels for a while. They'll see you later. You have a couple of first-degree burns and they've been treated. No concussion, just the smoke inhalation causing you to be disoriented before you passed out." He studied her intently. Funny, his eyes reminded her of Paul Newman's. Lorna would love Beau.

The burns began to sting, reminding her why she was here. "I remember going in," she told him. "The kennel was latched. The dogs couldn't have done it themselves. Someone took them." *God, let them be alive and well.* "When can I leave?"

"Doc said once you woke, he'd talk to you and then let us know."

"How did I get out of the house?"

Todd. Todd had carried her out. But that was impossible. Delusional. But she remembered kissing him, urging him to kiss her back, and he hadn't.

Because she hadn't been kissing Todd.

Heat bloomed in her chest, reaching all the way to the top of her head. "You," she whispered. "You rescued me. *You* told me to rest."

Beau looked away, distress scrunching his brows. "I did," he murmured.

Humiliation blanketed her and she drew her covers up. "I kissed you."

"I didn't kiss you back, Sissy. I knew you were…confused. I promise I didn't do—"

"I know." He'd told her he had her. To rest. And she had. But she'd been vulnerable. Told him things that she kept bone-deep. "I…um…"

He stood. "Sissy, please don't feel embarrassed or sorry. I—" He let it drop as if he couldn't find the words. Or didn't want to voice them. "I'll leave you to gather your thoughts. I'll go get a coffee, but I won't leave you."

She noticed his bandage again and reached out, taking a gentle hold of his hand. "Did you do this saving me?"

"It's not a big deal."

It was to her. "It wasn't smart to run into a fire. I know that. I never meant to put you at risk."

Beau squeezed her hand, then reluctantly released it. Approaching the door, he paused and pivoted, gazing into her eyes. "Sissy, I would run into a thousand fires for you."

FIVE

Beau sat inside the Spencer family's ranch. Worn and lived in like a family's house should be. Jackets hung over the kitchen chairs, and a few pairs of men's shoes lay haphazardly by the back door. He'd been telling himself he was going to get his own place. But his family ranch was so huge he had the east wing all to himself, with a kitchen to boot. Though he never used it. To be honest, he felt the place was a mausoleum. He hated it. Always had, even if he had boasted about its amenities as a teenager.

He'd loved this homey ranch.

These people.

Loved the realness.

He'd given Sissy a ride here about three hours ago. Silence had hung the entire way and her cheeks had been flushed. Could be from the fire. More likely, she was stewing in embarrassment. It wasn't like she had amnesia. Nor did he. He remembered in precise detail what happened inside her burning home.

She'd clung to him, kissed him and begged him to return the affection, the longing and the love. In her confused and vulnerable state, she'd revealed the greatest secrets of her heart.

Loneliness. Despair. Pain. Loss.

And her desire to connect again. To be loved and to love.

Beau hadn't been able to meet that need. She wasn't baring her soul to him. Sissy had been baring it to the man she loved and had lost. The man whom she desperately desired but could never see or touch or taste this side of heaven.

But it didn't matter that when he'd rushed in, terrified and panicked she might be dead, when he'd inhaled smoke until his lungs burned and felt the searing heat on his skin, she hadn't called out for him. Hadn't wanted him. All that mattered was she was alive.

Any hope of them being more than civil was enough for him. At one time, civility hadn't even been on the table. Maybe they could end up genuine friends. If she could forgive him and trust him again. He wasn't holding his breath.

Regardless of what might become—or not—he had to find this killer. Find her dogs. Sissy had already suffered insurmountable loss. She was hanging by a thread. A thinner thread than he'd once assumed. On the outside, it appeared that Sissy had been doing well, though what was the measure of well? She worked, she laughed, she smiled. But getting out of bed and going to work and being with family members didn't actually equate to healing. No, Sissy had stuffed down the truth. She was bearing grief alone.

He looked at his computer screen. He had some information that he needed, but still no word on Reggie or the work van he'd climbed inside. These past few hours he'd been researching while Sissy slept. Marisol had woken and he'd fixed her a sandwich all while listening to her protests. The chemo was doing a number on her energy levels. The least he could do was make her a turkey-and-avocado sandwich. She'd done so much for him over the years.

The back door opened and Sissy's brothers entered. Her eldest brother first. Stone still carried the confident swagger of a former Texas Ranger. His light brown hair was disheveled and his green eyes stayed in a perpetual scowl. Behind him, Bridge, who favored Stone minus the eye color, entered next, carrying on a conversation about baseball with Rhode, who brought up the rear. He and Sissy looked like their mom. Dark features. Bronzed skin. Midnight eyes.

Stone spotted him in the living room first and his scowl deepened. Stone had never been a fan of Beau's, and he had suspicions that Stone Spencer had more knowledge than the other brothers about his and Sissy's relationship and breakup. He had punched Beau in the nose. Truth be told,

Stone thought him a spoiled brat. He wasn't completely wrong. "Sissy asleep?" Stone asked.

Beau nodded. "Been out about four hours now, I think." He lifted his laptop. "I've been doing some work and Dom sent over a few cases that might match the MO."

"Me and my contacts at the FBI haven't found any dirt on Kiefer or anyone who might have a vendetta or grudge against him." Bridge plopped in the brown recliner and kicked off his shoes. "When you say matching MO, you mean a pattern? And how many cases? We just got over one serial killer in the Texas Hill Country. I'm not ready for another."

A door opening and closing halted the conversation as Sissy tiptoed into the living room. Her hair hung past her shoulders, thick and wet, and a pillow crease lined her left cheek. Man, she was beautiful. Inside and out.

The brothers gushed over her and finally she waved them off and sat beside Stone on the love seat, casting Beau a look that begged for his discretion. And for the first time he saw a measure of calm with him being in the room.

All eyes were on him. Not as Beau the son of a Texan multimillionaire oilman, but Beau the private investigator, a professional, an equal. He'd never felt like he measured up to a Spencer. Until maybe now. Or at least close to measuring up. Pride swelled in his chest and confidence moved him forward. "As I was saying… The guy is smart. He's avoided targeting couples in the same county and spread out his time between accident/kills, which has kept him off the law enforcement radar. Our first victim of an accidental death was James Beardon. Welder. Was working on a wrought iron staircase and fell down the stairs, broke his neck, before his wedding. Over in Hays County. Eight months later, the woman he was going to marry was strangled in a hotel in Austin. Taser marks on her neck."

"That's awful," Sissy said.

Beau nodded. "It is, but there was no reason to connect it to the 'accidental' death of her fiancé. Case went cold six years ago."

"Next?" Stone asked.

"Don Breckin, a thrill junkie. Parachute failed and he fell to his death four weeks before his wedding to Babs Arlington. A year after Don's death, Babs was smothered with her feather pillow on her couch. Taser marks on her right side. Five years ago. Case cold in Blanco County."

"No one thought to put these two together?" Bridge frowned.

"Why? Two men died tragically a year apart in different ways. Two different counties. The only connection in the database was the Taser marks. Manner of death wasn't the same and killers typically do things the same way each time."

"How many more Tasered women came up in

the system who also had a significant other die tragically earlier?" Rhode asked.

"One," Beau said. "Richard Buxton, a mechanic. Jack collapsed and the car fell on him six weeks before his wedding to Rolanda Meeks. Who was also found strangled on her kitchen floor. This was a year and a half after Richard's death. Taser marks on her lower back. I emailed you what I have, Rhode."

"What county was this in?" Stone asked.

"Ours. This makes two here, counting Kiefer and my sister," he said, but the words didn't feel real to him.

"Not quite a year, a year and over a year. Why such a difference in time?" Rhode asked. "You're right. He's clever and calculated. Using ways to kill the men that would make sense to who they were, what they did for a living or hobbies they enjoyed. Fell down the stairs doing a welding job. Parachute failure. Mechanical error. But the women—he murders them and doesn't mind that anyone knows it. He makes physical contact with them, unlike with the men."

Stone stood and paced. "Forced entry in any of the cases?"

"No. And no camera footage from the hotel where our first female victim was murdered. I checked already," Beau said.

"We know he left the thumb drive at Coco's, and based on what Sissy said was on the video, he talked to his victims. Wanted them to see the footage he shot months and even over a year earlier. Talk about a patient killer." Stone took a moment to think. "If our theory is correct, and he used a Taser to subdue the women, how did he make them watch that footage without another struggle?"

"There were struggles with them. Even my sister. I think he got in and used the video footage to control them. I'd sit down to see something about someone I loved that was gone."

"I know I would," Sissy murmured.

"Then, after they panicked, knowing they were going to die—he said so on the video— the struggle occurred and the Taser incapacitated them enough to smother or strangle them." Beau ground his teeth at the thought.

"Good work," Rhode said. "We need to talk with the families of these victims. Maybe we can find a connection linking them all to one person or place that will help us drill down and find the killer."

"I'd like to know if this man might have dated these women and was jilted by them. Revenge would be killing their new loves and then ultimately them. He'd want to see them suffer." Bridge toyed with a remote on the arm of the recliner.

"It's pain." Sissy finally spoke. "Those photos… Forcing Coco to see them would bring her complete pain and suffering. If what Stone suspects is true of the other victims, then maybe he wanted the women to relive the death of their loved one so he could watch. Why else take photos of them at their most vulnerable times? The funeral, graveside and subsequent visits. There were no pictures taken other than the ones that dealt with her pain of loss."

The room fell silent.

Beau struggled to absorb the vileness of this kind of act, to try to come to terms with a person who could do such a thing. Why? Why would someone enjoy seeing another human being suffer over loss and grief?

"I think we might need some help working up a profile," Stone said. "My friend Tack Holliday works for the Texas Rangers and his wife, Chelsey, owns a private consulting firm with two other former behavioral analysts with the FBI. We should call her."

Beau nodded. This was much bigger than them. They could investigate and theorize all day long, but a professional who did this for a living was worth talking to. "I agree. We need all the help we can muster."

Sissy was a target and now her dogs were missing. He'd call out the National Guard if he thought they'd come keep her safe and find this nasty killer.

Rhode stood. "I'll take the first two victims.

Beau, you work the one in our county…and Co-co's. You'll know her friends and people she was connected to. Sissy, you can help him with that. Coco probably confided things in you that she didn't to anyone else. And we'll find Lady and Louie. The guy didn't let them burn. He might have a sensitive spot for pooches."

A man who was sadistic toward humans but would save a dog from a burning fire. Great.

"I don't care if he is taking care of them. They'll be afraid, and I don't want him near my babies!" She balled a fist. "We have to find him. Find my dogs."

"I'll call Tack," Stone said and stood. "And about tonight—"

Beau raised a hand. He'd been thinking about this since Coco had been attacked. "Coco would want you to go ahead with this evening. I haven't canceled anything and you shouldn't either." Stone had planned a birthday party for Emily and was going to surprise her by proposing. Just because life was coming to a halt for many didn't mean it should for everyone. They had to keep moving forward. Coco would definitely want that. Want them to have a night to celebrate life. It was too fragile and short not to.

Stone looked at his brothers and at Sissy. "Are y'all in agreement? Things are escalating. First Coco, now Sissy. And—"

"Stone," Sissy said, interrupting him. "You've

been waiting to start your life with Emily—to take it to the forever stage, and I think you should."

"I agree," Rhode said.

"Same," Bridge added. "I have a buddy in the Bureau who might be able to lend a hand. I'll make a call." Bridge left the room, and then Stone and Rhode followed.

Beau turned to Sissy. "Do you want to rest and start tomorrow?"

"No. Time is wasting," Sissy insisted. "Let's get started now. Get some traction before tonight's party."

Sissy did not want to attend the birthday party at the Brighton mansion this evening. Not because she didn't want to celebrate Emily's birthday or the engagement, but her dogs were still missing and she was a nervous wreck. She'd prayed off and on throughout the day that God would give her peace, but so far, she'd had zero peace. Instead, she'd stewed and worried and kept it inside.

Since Beau was her chauffeur and babysitter, she'd had him take her to the training facility earlier. She kept an office there and she wanted to tell the staff firsthand what had happened. She'd been working with Brad since before Todd died, training therapy dogs while he trained in protection and obedience. When Abe and Cherie came on board, Abe specialized in obedience and Cherie in medical support. They were like family, especially after Todd was killed.

After leaving the training facility, they'd driven into Austin to interview the family of the third victim—Richard Buxton, the mechanic. According to them, he and Rolanda Meeks had been in love since high school, but Rolanda wanted to get her master's degree in English before marrying and having children. His family said he was a careful mechanic and found it hard to believe he'd go under the car with a wobbly jack, but that was what appeared to have happened.

Beau hadn't offered any answer other than he'd been hired to look into a recent murder and it might connect to Rolanda Meeks's murder, which led them to Richard. He wanted to keep the fact they were on to the killer quiet and Sissy had agreed. If it had been an accident after all, there was no point in causing new grief to the family members. They'd driven back to Cedar Springs, where Rolanda Meeks's family lived, and her parents told the same story. After Richard's death, they didn't think Rolanda would ever come out of the grief fog, even with the counseling and support group she'd attended in Austin.

Sissy had related. No one understood better the depression, anger and fear or the uncertainty of the future. But then Rolanda slowly emerged, a more hopeful person who was ready to take it one hour at a time into a new normal, if it could be called that. Sissy understood that too. Mrs. Meeks had shown them photo albums of Rolanda and Richard—their love for one another radiating in each smile. They'd bought a house, a dog and even a boat in preparation for married life and the adventures they wanted to take—most of them at the lake, based on the purchases and their love for the outdoors.

When asked about Rolanda's murder, her mother admitted that Rolanda had confessed she felt watched over the months after Richard died. She never spotted anyone; it was just a feeling, especially on the days she'd visited Richard's grave or when she entered or exited the grief support group. She had no enemies. No one her family could think of who might have held a grudge.

A soft knock drew her from thoughts of the day's work and she called out permission to enter. Even though she was residing in her childhood bedroom, she had no clothes except a few items. Everything in her home was either burned or ruined from the smoke.

Her soon-to-be sister-in-law, Emily, eased into the room, her fiery red hair hanging in waves over her shoulders and her intense brown eyes scrutinizing Sissy. She was dressed in dark jeans, boots and a soft green sweater.

Sissy had liked Emily from the moment Stone arrived on the family ranch to keep her safe due to a deadly case she was working in the Public Integrity Unit of the Texas Rangers. They'd become fast friends and sisters. Sissy's actual older sister, Paisley, would have loved Emily too—especially the way she riled up Stone—but she'd been murdered over four years ago. No, the Spencer family was no stranger to loss, grief and hardship.

"I wanted to check on you. Personally." Emily closed the door with a quiet click. "How are you holding up?"

No point lying. Em was a top-notch Texas Ranger and would easily know if Sissy was lying. "Not well. I miss my dogs. I hurt for Coco. And I'm scared."

Emily hugged her and rubbed her back. "It is scary. I was out of my mind when I was being hunted down by a killer, and I'm trained for dealing with them. No shame in being afraid. We're going to do everything in our power to find him, and your dogs. I know how much you love them."

"I do. After losing Annabelle, they've become my children. And I'm sorry if I'll seem distracted tonight at your birthday party. I don't want to be."

Emily smiled. "Anyone would be. I told Stone we should cancel, and Beau too, but they say Coco would want it this way. I don't know her well, but what else can I do but agree? I'm not a party person in general and Stone knows this. Stone himself would rather pick up tacos and stay in and watch a movie."

"He's always been a homebody."

"I'm not complaining." Emily sighed. "I checked on your mom. She's getting dressed and ready, but I can tell she's zapped and not feeling well. It's just a birthday party."

Sissy cocked her head. Emily was savvy and intuitive. The signs of this being more than a birthday party were all there. Was she playing dumb to give Stone and the rest of them the joy of the surprise? That would fit her character.

"Why are you looking at me like that?" Emily eyed Sissy with suspicion and then Sissy saw it. The truth. Emily knew exactly what was up tonight.

Sissy grinned. "You're good."

Emily winked. "Well, of course I am. It's my job and Stone is the worst liar on the planet. But I don't want to spoil all his hard work. Still amazes me he doesn't realize I'm expecting a proposal based on a comment he made to me Christmas morning when he asked when my birthday was. But all in good fun."

"Have y'all talked about where you'll live? I mean, of course you can stay here, but y'all might want a little more privacy." She grinned and winked back.

"Your mom needs us. But we've discussed some options. Building a smaller cabin for the two of us on the property—away from Bridge.

Sometimes you make things work even when it's not ideal."

Sissy nodded. "I don't know if the insurance will pay out or not since it's arson. Either way, I have no idea when I'll be able to move out of here. I'll try to be gone by the wedding bells." For their privacy and because it was too much to see a happy honeymooning couple without the ache in her own hollow chest.

"Sissy, did you hear what I just said? You do what needs done for family. It'll all work. God always takes the bad and brings it about for good if we let Him."

Sissy hadn't seen the good in the deaths of her husband and child. But she kept silent. There was no good there. None. "We'll figure it out."

Emily eyed her long enough to make her squirm, then left her to finish getting ready for tonight. Jeans. Sweater. Easy. She wore her hair up in a messy bun but pulled a few tendrils down to frame her face and added large gold hoops to dress it up. After a little mascara and some tinted gloss, she headed downstairs, where Beau stood in the living room, hands jammed in his pockets, working his lips in a nervous twist.

She paused and let herself take a few seconds to really look at him. Dressed in dark, trendy jeans, a white dress shirt and gray sports coat, the man could never make casual look anything but male model worthy. Looks and money. He had both.

Her stomach corkscrewed and she clutched it. She hadn't had a visceral reaction to a man since Todd died. Since he'd passed, her life was like dry deadwood, drifting along on a river to nowhere. Why did her reaction have to rear up when gazing on Beau Brighton?

He must have realized she was in the room. He slowly turned and straightened the lapels of his sports coat while casting a long glance on her. He held her gaze and the corkscrew belly went into action again. A wild roller coaster.

Finally, he said, "You ready?"

Was she ready? Sissy couldn't even describe what she was feeling, but that one word felt ripe. She was not ready, not for the weird emotions surfacing. Not for Beau in general. But she said yes anyway.

After grabbing her purse and the birthday gift from a table, she looked up and Beau was staring at her. She did not like the expression. Soft and torn. The look he'd given her so many times when they were teenagers. The one that made her feel like no other woman existed. And if they did, he had no idea they walked the planet. She was his focus. His object of affection. His world.

And she'd fallen headlong into that emotion and into him.

It had gotten her burned.

But she wasn't making that mistake again.

"What's in the box?" he asked and closed the distance between them. She caught the subtle hint of his cologne. Expensive. Exquisite. Enthralling.

Her mouth turned to dust. "Uh…it's a white Stetson. For work. Practical but she'll like it."

"Here, let me carry that," Beau said and leaned in, and her breath caught. He paused and peered down at her. "You okay?" he murmured.

No. Not in the least. Why did he have to be so handsome and smell good, and why did he have to be so stinking kind and gentle?

"You have a date tonight for the party?" she blurted. Why else would he go to such lengths to look and smell amazing?

He cocked his head, puzzlement on his face. "No. Was I supposed to?"

"When have you never had someone on your arm?" she asked with a roll of her eyes. It was far easier and safer to be combative than kind. "And…you smell nice is all. Seemed like you went to extra trouble."

His full lips spread into an irresistible grin that showed off his boyish dimples. Why were rich men so good-looking? Was it a requirement or something? "I really don't think cleaning up and smelling nice is extra trouble. Are you saying I normally stink?"

"No," she said and felt the heat balloon in her chest. "I just… I don't know." She stomped to the door and swung it open, heading for his car. He followed right behind.

Inside the car, he buckled up and said, "And I do have someone on my arm tonight. Just not a date."

"Well, I don't mean to kill your game."

He blew a long, quiet breath and shifted to look her in the eye. "Sissy, I have no game. Not anymore. And I'm not sure how great it was then."

It wasn't so much his game as his good looks and confident swagger, and his money never hurt. But those were always shallow girls. "You ever date anyone who actually knew you? Like really knew you?"

Beau adjusted the radio to country pop and turned it down low, then pulled out of the drive. A grimace twisted his brow. "Once," he murmured. "But I thought you knew that."

Once she would have said she'd known him better than himself. But he'd lied. It had all been an act. Tell her what she wanted to hear to get what he wanted to have.

Except that wasn't true. He didn't get what she didn't willingly give. But she'd been manipulated with the lies and the good-guy act.

It'd felt real, though.

They drove in silence until they reached the long drive leading up to the Brighton estate. "Beau?"

"Hmm?"

Lorna Landoon was right. She deserved to know the truth no matter what the truth turned out to be. "Why did you give me the cold shoulder after…after what happened between us? What happened was wrong, but you had no guilty conscience about that. So why?"

Beau slowed the car and glanced at her. "Why do you think I did what I did?"

Sissy sighed. She'd done stepped into it now. No going back. "I think you wanted one thing from me and knew you had to go about it another way than your normal conquests who were impressed with your money and good looks. I never was. I mean, your looks never hurt but… I'd fallen in love with you—the person I thought you were."

His eyebrows rose and nostrils flared. "I see. Wow. I don't really have a response to that, Sissy. Sorry." His Adam's apple bobbed and he sped up and parked, allowing the valet to attend his fancy sports car so he didn't have to park it himself.

Had she hurt his feelings? Angered him? Well, he'd done all those things to her and he was dancing around his answer like a politician.

She stepped out and waited on him. "What else do you expect me to think?"

"I guess nothing." He hesitated, then gave her his arm to guide her up the steps. She reluctantly looped hers through it.

Inside the foyer, a table was filled with gifts

wrapped in a variety of colorful paper. Beau added the gift Sissy had brought. She recognized friends, family—including Emily's half sister, Dottie, and her half brother, but she couldn't remember his name. Music filtered through unseen speakers and the food table was covered with tacos and chips and guacamole along with churros.

Sissy's stomach growled and she was surprised she could eat. She made a plate and Beau followed suit. The guest of honor and Stone entered, and they sang her "Happy Birthday." Stone had never looked so happy. It was a beautiful night for them.

Lady A's ballad "What If I Never Get Over You" began as she and Beau stood by and watched couples and friends slip onto the outdoor brick dance floor where they held parties and outdoor cooking classes.

Twinkling lights had been strung above the wooden rafters and three firepits warmed the air, knocking off the night chill.

"You…you want to dance?" he asked, uncertain.

"Do you want to give me a straight answer?" she countered.

He nodded once and held out his hand for her to accept.

She placed her hand in his unbandaged hand and he led her to the edge of the floor where only firelight glowed and privacy abounded. He arrested her gaze and slowly pulled her against him, then slid his arm around the small of her back. A heady feeling came over her and then he drew her flush against him. "This okay?" he whispered.

She nodded, unable to speak.

Gripping his shoulder, resting her head right under his chin, she noticed his neck. A neck she'd peppered with gentle kisses. She felt his arms around her. The same arms she'd felt protected and safe in yesterday. Arms that felt stronger than she'd remembered them feeling.

She closed her eyes and held back feverish tears. How could she feel this way in the arms of another man who wasn't her late husband?

How could it be Beau's? After all he'd done to break her.

But she did. Her heart screamed she wasn't just in arms that could protect her from danger but she was in a safe place in every way.

That couldn't be true, though.

Could it?

She pulled back, searching his eyes and trying to figure out what on earth was happening to her and was it happening to him? She desperately hoped it wasn't. He didn't look away and they slowly turned and moved with the rhythm of the song. His hand slid from her lower back to her upper back, holding her in place as if he feared she'd bolt any second, and she was contemplating it.

"I was afraid, Sissy," he finally said. "Straight answer. I was afraid I'd end up ruining us—ruining you even further than I did that night. I was eighteen. Terrified and in love. I had no idea how to explain what I was feeling and I had too much pride to admit I'd done wrong by you and that I was weak. That my dad was right about me. I did the only thing I knew how to do to protect myself—and, in a twisted sense of logic, protect you from me."

"I thought you could tell me anything."

"I wanted to be someone who could make you proud, Sissy. I'd failed you. I should have shown some restraint."

"I didn't say no. I clearly remember saying yes."

"Doesn't matter. I saw our life flash before my eyes and then I saw me breaking you down the road. So I did what I thought I had to. I pretended I didn't care. Pretended you meant nothing."

Sissy couldn't control her trembling lip, but she was holding back tears with all she had.

"Truth is, Sissy, you meant everything to me. I regret losing control and I regret how I handled it."

"I regret what happened too." Betraying her, a tear slipped over the edge and spilled onto her cheek.

Beau's thumb softly brushed it away. "I don't regret having loved you, though. And I did. If I'm lying I'm dying, Sissy. I *loved* you."

A volcano of emotion erupted in her throat. She'd asked for the truth. She wasn't prepared for this. "I loved you too."

"Not as much as I loved you. There's no way."

He had no reason to lie. There was nothing to gain. And as she peered into his eyes, she knew he was laying down nothing but the truth. Finally.

Fear of his feelings and fear of failing her even more had motivated his behavior. It was still wrong, but who knew? Back then, before he'd been a man of faith, he might have ruined them.

But he'd loved her. He'd meant those words. Meant it in his kiss. In his touch. In his actions. Without thinking it through, she rose up on her toes and pressed a kiss to his lips. Wanting to feel them, knowing exactly whom she was kissing this time.

But he pulled away and placed his index finger on her mouth. "I can't," he whispered. "I mean, I won't. Not like this. Not when you're vulnerable and afraid."

Words she'd confessed to him thinking he was Todd.

"Because I don't want to make a mistake, Sissy. And more importantly, I don't want to be a mistake." He swallowed. "Maybe in the past, a year ago even, I would have. I'd have kissed you senseless because I wanted to. I've never not wanted to kiss you. But now things are different. I want something behind it besides nostalgia or a really perfect moment with music and firelight."

She was rejected by him again, but at least this time she understood. Granted, she was surprised. But Beau, for once, was right. She *was* lonely. She *was* confused. She *was* emotional and vulnerable. She *was* caught up in a romantic perfect moment.

She still missed Todd. Wanted him. How could she possibly kiss another man when she hadn't let go of her husband? Probably never could or would. "You're right. I'm sorry."

"I am too." His lips grazed her brow as the song ended. "If you'll excuse me..." He strode from the dance floor toward the stables. His place to think.

The squeak of a microphone drew her from the moment, from watching him walk away again. Stone took the stage and stumbled through a beautiful speech and heartfelt proposal to Emily.

Sissy applauded but inside she ached.

"God, what is happening?" Beau asked as he kicked around the stables. He'd been out here doing the same thing the night the chief of staff's wife had been killed at Christmastime and his wallet had been left behind, implicating him as her murderer. Those memories ignited a shiver in his bones. Why was his life going off the rails now? Hadn't he given his life to Christ and professed Him as Lord and Savior? And yet everything around him was falling apart and his heart was in deep turmoil.

It was more than regrets and the wondering of what if. Something else was brewing. Maybe it was due to forced proximity. Or his fear over her life. He couldn't pinpoint it and wasn't sure he wanted to.

Her lips on his skin as he carried her from her burning house… He could feel them now, pressed against him. He'd been tempted to give in to the moment, to surrender to how she'd made him feel. But for once he'd denied himself.

Then she'd broken his heart with her words. Words of loneliness, exhaustion and fear. All he'd wanted to do was give her rest, peace and strength, but that was above his pay grade. Beau was rich, yet he didn't have what it would take to give her those things.

His money and privilege hadn't given him those things either. He'd only found rest, peace and strength in his Savior. And even then—like now—he was feeling anxious and unsettled…and weak. He was weak. Always had been.

Once they solved the case, caught the killer and Sissy wasn't cemented to him 24/7, his bones would settle, the fire would stop raging and he'd find his own peace. Because Sissy wasn't over her husband. And Beau wouldn't, couldn't, be a surrogate.

Even if none of that was a factor, he couldn't be sure he'd be right for her. What if he messed it up? What if he failed her? Failed them both? "God, give me strength and help me to fight these feelings. Take them away. Please," he murmured, and the horses stirred in their stalls at his presence.

Raking his hand through his hair, he sighed, then trudged back to the party. He was happy for Stone and Emily. He'd always wondered if Stone would remain a bachelor. Bridge once had Wendy, but that... Well, she'd disappeared and everyone suspected she'd run off with a man she'd been in love with before meeting Bridge. The Spencer family had been racked by loss and grief, yet they stood firm in their faith. He aspired to that kind of life. One that wouldn't be blown around by the storms that life brewed but stood solid in faith. Anchored in hope. Even in times like when his dad was overt in his disappointment in him. When his parents' marriage turned chilly. When, like right now, his own feet were touched to fire and he was unsure if he could handle everything barreling toward him.

"Lord, help me catch this killer. Not for a win in my life but for Sissy. She needs a win. She needs a breather, Lord. The whole family does."

He reentered the party, where people were

dancing, eating and enjoying the evening. He wished Coco was here. He'd checked in with the nurses' station earlier and there was no change. Mom had called and said she'd be flying in at the end of the week, but Dad had more business to attend to. Figured.

Sissy danced with Stone, locked into a deeply somber conversation. She glanced up and caught his eye, then slipped away from her brother's arms as his fiancée jumped right into them. The way Emily looked at Stone… Beau wanted that. He wanted to be looked at as if he was the only one in the world. A look that revealed deep, abiding love and a hope for a long future.

Sissy approached. "I told Stone I was feeling a little tired. Besides, Mama left right after the engagement. Rhode took her but he's been back about half an hour. I think I'll go see to her and try to sleep. Would you mind taking me back to the ranch?"

"Not at all."

"About earlier…"

"Water under the bridge." He stopped and shook his head. "I hate that phrase. It sounds like I'm gonna drown your brother."

She snickered. "I think you've been suspected of being a serial killer enough without adding this new MO."

"Amen." He laughed. "Come on. Let's go

get your purse and I'll drive you back and stick around until one of your brothers shows up."

After they collected her purse and the valet brought his car around, Beau opened the sunroof. The night was chilly but not cold, and the stars twinkled like diamonds overhead. It was a near perfect evening minus the sore heart and hopelessness of ever being with Sissy Spencer. "You don't mind the sunroof, do you?"

"No. I like it." She picked at fake lint on her jeans. "I'm worried about my dogs. And the fact they haven't found your security booth guy—Reggie?"

"Yeah. No van. No Reggie. I had the staff send a card and flowers to his wife, but that feels trite. I didn't know what else to do. He's either collateral damage or involved. Either way, it stinks for Marilyn."

"It's hard to lose your husband. Maybe I can offer her some assistance. I know how to talk the talk. But as you well know now, I can't seem to walk the walk."

Beau glanced over. "Tell me how you two met." This would hurt. But she needed it. She needed the good memories. Something to make her smile. Beau was not her ray of sunshine. Todd Weils was. And he could not compete with a dead man's memories.

Sissy grinned. A real grin confirming what he already knew to be true. He'd endure tiny flecks of pain to see her shine like this. "It was raining and I was running across campus to the library. His raincoat hood was obstructing his view and he barreled into me like a linebacker, knocking me flat on my bum and my books went into a puddle. I was ticked off beyond belief. Books weren't cheap."

Beau laughed, picturing anyone knocking over a fighter like Sissy. "And you gave him a mouthful, am I right?"

"You better believe it." She laughed. "And the next day a brand-new textbook was sitting in front of my dorm door with a card. He apologized and hoped we could start over, same time, same place that night. So, I showed up."

"That's a great story." And it was. "Was it love instantly?"

Sissy sighed. "No. I, uh... I hemmed and hawed about even showing up. We became friends first. That's all I could offer, and even that was difficult. Todd was patient, and after a year I went on my first date with him. Six months in I think I truly trusted him. And three months later he proposed. He'd wanted to for a while, but...he was waiting for it to rain." She sniffed.

"I'm sorry. I didn't mean to bring up pain."

She shook her head. "No. No, you didn't. It's happy tears. Really."

Beau squirmed in his seat, knowing that he was to blame for Sissy's trepidation in falling in love. In trusting. "I'm sorry. I didn't realize the effect what I did would have—or at least how far it would reach."

"I believe you."

He waited a beat. "He proposed in the rain? At the library?"

"He did." She beamed and sighed happily. "We were married that next spring. But you know that."

"I do."

The car swirled with silence. He didn't offer how he'd been tempted to tell her how he felt about her at the wedding. That would go to the grave with him.

Lights shone in the rearview, getting his attention and causing him to squint his eyes. "Dude, turn off the brights already," he grumbled.

"I don't know why people do that," Sissy said.

They appeared to be getting brighter.

No. Closer.

Before Beau could utter a word, the vehicle rammed into them, lurching his car forward. Beau lost control of the wheel and the car swerved into the other lane on the isolated stretch of highway. He grabbed hold and brought it back before it careened into the deep ditch.

This road was nothing but hills and stretches of pastureland.

Sissy shrieked. And he feared she was reliving

that horrible car accident they'd gotten into when she'd lost her family in an instant.

"Hang tight!" He white-knuckled the wheel, but the truck behind them was big enough to crush his sports car. His only hope was he could outrun him.

Slamming on the gas, he heard the big engine roar as they bulleted forward, but the truck must have a hemi engine, because unfortunately it kept up.

Inching up beside the driver's side, the truck slammed into them. Beau felt it from head to toe and the car skidded across the lane and straight for the steep ditch.

Beau lost control.

The car went airborne and crashed down with a sickening thud, then sailed through barbed wire fencing into a cow pasture. Sissy screeched as the airbag deployed. The car came to a stop about five feet from a huge pond, and Beau's airbag broke through, stinging his face upon impact and dazing him.

"Sissy, are you hurt?" He shoved the airbag down as it deflated.

She undid her seat belt and touched her neck. The seat belt had dug into her skin and she was bleeding. She had a few facial abrasions from the airbag. But thankfully, she was okay. "I think I'm good. My neck hurts but I can move it."

They both were going to feel it later. "We have to run. Now. This was no accident."

She nodded and opened her door, stumbling out.

"Easy," he called and clambered out of the car, rushing around the hood to get to her. "You dizzy?"

"No. Just…wobbly. I can walk. It's the adrenaline."

He wrapped his arm around her waist. "Let's get out of here."

Gunfire erupted, and the sound of bullets hitting his car sent a wave of panic into his chest.

"Stay down and run!"

SIX

Sissy bolted from the car that was being shot at and then flattened herself into the pasture like a pancake, her heart rate spiking to dangerous levels. Other than hills and a few sparse trees, they had no protection.

The shooter would come right down the hill and find them at any moment. She already saw a light shining above.

"Do you have your phone?" Sissy asked. Hers was in her purse in the car and going back was suicide.

"I had it in the console and couldn't find it when we bolted from the car."

So much for calling the cops or anyone.

Beau laid a hand on her upper back. "We've got to shoot our way out."

"We only have your one gun. We don't know how many guns he has. Plus, what if he shoots the gas tank and blows up the car? We aren't that far from it."

Beau scanned the area with a grimace as if

trying to come up with a new plan. "Okay, stay low and follow me."

They raced from the car that could be used as a bomb, staying crouched, and headed right for the massive pond.

"What exactly are you planning, Beau? This isn't a cartoon. We're not going to find a hollow reed to help us breathe underwater."

"I love that you think my ideas come from old episodes of *Looney Tunes*, Sissy." His voice was flat and unamused.

"Then what are we doing?"

A gun fired and Sissy winced. Then they froze.

"He doesn't know we've left the car," Beau whispered. "He's hoping to flush us out into the open, which means he has no idea where we are."

Yet.

"See that johnboat overturned by the water's edge?"

"You want to climb in a boat and go out on the pond? That's a terrible idea, Beau. Talk about shooting fish in a barrel."

"No. Let's get *under* the boat."

"But it's at the edge of water and it's spring, which means there'll be snakes," she hissed. "And what if he finds us?"

"Then we'll have no choice but to shoot. There's no gas tank. Not even a trolling motor. It's our only chance, Sissy."

"Fine." Crouching, she raced down to the water's edge, the smell of earth, fish and decay slamming into her nostrils. Beau raised the boat. The ground was muddy and soaked with at least an inch of water mixed with twigs and who knew what. But she dropped and lay on her back. Beau settled in and let the boat canopy them.

Cold water seeped through the back of her clothing and drenched her hair. She shivered and tried not to think about snakes and spiders and other creeping things she detested. "What if he starts shooting the boat without checking first?"

"Nah. He doesn't have an arsenal of guns. He'd be stupid to shoot blindly. I'm aimed and ready. We'll hear him coming and he'll have to lift the boat. Takes two hands. We'll be ready."

She hoped Beau knew what he was talking about. She'd start shooting through the boat if it was her. But his tone sounded confident. She prayed he was right.

The cluster of trees rustled and a tiny beam of light peeked through the crack between the boat and the ground. Sissy held her breath and kept praying.

Another round of gunfire erupted. She flinched but kept her scream buried in her chest. Beau squeezed her hand. Time felt like it was eking by, but she had no idea how long they lay there, breathing, holding hands and clinging on to hope. The light had disappeared but the gunman could have switched it off, waiting them out. They had no idea.

"I'm freezing," she said.

"Me too. I'm going to lift the boat and slide out, then go check. You stay here no matter what. You understand? Shots. Screams. Whatever. You stay here and you stay safe."

"Beau, what if—"

"Promise me."

What choice did she have? "Fine. I promise. But like…don't die."

"I'll do my best."

She felt his lips graze her brow; then the boat lifted, a rush of cool air adding to her already frozen and wet state. Beau slipped out and light beamed in, but once the boat concealed her, darkness enveloped her. Nothing but the scent of stagnant water and rotten fish.

Questions circled her brain as time passed.

Surely by now this guy knew she'd told the police everything. Why keep coming after her?

Where was Beau?

No gunfire had erupted since he left her here alone.

"Sissy," Beau called quietly. "It's me. He's gone. A car slowed. I'm guessing the driver thought he might be having car trouble, so he sped off."

Relief flooded her system as Beau pulled the

johnboat off her and helped her stand. She was covered in mud and her clothing was soaked. "It's safe?"

"For now. I'm grateful to the Lord for that other vehicle."

"Amen," she said and followed Beau up the hill to the road.

"I found my cell phone and your purse." He handed it to her. "I called your cousin Dom and Rhode. Dom will want a statement and Rhode's gonna give us a lift to the house."

Sissy shivered. "I'm freezing."

"That's why I said to the house—my place. You can use the guest room, and I asked Rita to snag some clothes from Coco's closet. She won't mind. We'll get you dry and warm before taking you home."

She was grateful to Beau and his house manager. His house was closer than her own and she was mud-caked. Even her hair was covered and weighing heavy on her head.

Beau called a tow truck for the car while they waited on Dom and Rhode.

Finally, blue lights flashed, signaling Dom. The headlights behind him revealed Rhode. They hopped out of the ditch and raced to the edge of the road, where they stood shaking.

"Everyone in one piece?" Rhode asked.

Dom turned his nose up at Sissy. "You look terrible, coz."

"Thanks." She tossed him a wry grin.

They gave Dom official statements; then the tow truck arrived and hauled off the car.

"I have some old towels and a blanket in the car. Let me lay it down before y'all get in," Rhode said. "You smell too. Not sure how to mask that."

Beau cut Sissy an amused eye. "*This* is why I wear cologne. You never know what you'll need to mask."

Sissy giggled, shocked she could. After Rhode situated the blanket and towels on the seat, Beau motioned for Sissy to climb in first. Then Rhode circled them back to the Brighton ranch. The place was quiet, all the birthday guests now gone, including Stone and Emily.

"Let's go in through the mudroom so Rita doesn't have both our hides."

Rita met them in the mudroom and mother-henned Sissy to the guest room. After cleaning up and drying her hair, Sissy came downstairs in a pair of sweats and an oversize Chanel sweatshirt that Coco loved. It made her feel close to her friend.

She found Beau in the massive kitchen, all stainless steel, marble and brick. He had a variety of luncheon meats laid out along with sides and condiments and several kinds of bread. "Near death makes me hungry," Beau said and licked a dot of mayo from his thumb. "How about you?"

"I eat my emotions in sweets."

"They left a good amount of birthday cake."

"Do you have ice cream?"

"Most definitely." He opened the freezer. "Vanilla, chocolate, butter pecan, rocky road or strawberry?"

"Good grief. You own stock in Ben and Jerry's?"

"No, but we should. We just like ice cream."

"You don't say?" She snickered and pointed. "I'll take plain vanilla and a slice of chocolate cake."

Beau nodded. "Nice."

They went to work making their food and then carried it outside under the covered patio, where the fire still blazed in the outdoor fireplace. Beau sat beside her on the love seat. "Did you have any spiders in your hair?"

"No, just mud and slime. You?"

"No. Just mud and slime."

They ate quietly, the fudgy icing pairing perfectly with the vanilla ice cream. But the indulgence of chocolate cake and ice cream didn't make the threat go away. She still felt every bit of tension in her stomach. "Why is he still after me? The cops know what's up and he has to know that too. Why can't he leave me alone?"

"I don't know, Sissy. Maybe you pose a fun challenge to him. He wants to follow through with what he started." He shook his head as he tore off a piece of crust from his bread. "I wish I knew."

"I've noticed you haven't given up and moved on either. And your life has repeatedly been on the line."

Beau set his plate on the wicker coffee table, his sandwich half eaten, and shifted to look her square in the eye. "I'm not quitting. Not this job, and not my promise to keep you safe and find who did this to Coco and is doing this to you now."

"I believe you," she whispered.

"You do?"

She nodded. "I had my doubts at first. Not now." Maybe he was made for this job. Beau had been nothing but courageous and compassionate, and he had a keen sense of deduction.

Beau's phone rang and he grimaced. "It's Dom." He answered and put it on speaker.

"Hey, we found the white van from the security footage," Dom said. "Stolen plates. A guy in Austin reported them stolen two days before Coco's attack. Some fishermen found the van in a lake on the edge of town."

Sissy pushed away her cake and ice cream.

"And Reggie?" Beau asked. "Did you find him too?"

"We did," Dom said. "He's dead."

Beau rubbed his eyes and poured another cup of coffee. After taking Sissy to her family ranch last night, he'd driven home but couldn't sleep.

Reggie was gone.

This morning, he'd called the Brighton attorney and seen to it that trusts were set up for Reggie's kids and his wife. The least he could do was make sure the family was financially stable. Later today, he'd go by and see his wife in person. Hopefully, the police would find prints or trace evidence in the van that would provide a lead to the killer, but Beau wasn't optimistic. This guy had possibly gotten away with killing eight people. He could only hope and pray that Coco would pull through.

Before calling their attorney, he'd called the nurses' station at the hospital. No updated information on his sister. Mom was arriving later today and planned to go straight to the hospital, where he'd meet her later. For now, he perched on a chair at the kitchen table with files, his laptop and one more cup of strong coffee.

He'd done some digging into the lives of the past victims. Their Facebook pages had been memorialized—a feature Facebook had been providing for a few years. One good thing about social media.

He'd been taking notes, hoping to find a connection through friends, family, employment and even recreational activities that might give them a place to start, but these couples had been vastly different in age, occupations and even entertainment choices. But he kept looking. All he needed was one common link.

His hand ached from the pages of notes on each victim. He'd scoured every nook and cranny of the internet hunting down information—even tidbits that seemed irrelevant. Now he spread them across the formal dining table, highlighting any similarities he could find.

Two of the women had pictures on social media of them swimming. Neither had visited the same pools that he noticed, but he highlighted it anyway.

Next, he put their engagement photos together. Not many couples did engagement photos in newspapers, but…wait a second. Hold on. He clapped his hands and did a victory pump with his fists in the air.

Beau had found a common link.

Finally.

Checking his watch, he clucked his tongue against his teeth. Time had slipped away from him. He'd started before the sun rose and now it was almost nine thirty. Rhode was taking Sissy to work at ten thirty, and it was Beau's job to meet him there and take over protection detail while she trained emotional therapy dogs. He couldn't imagine how hard it would be for Sissy to be around dogs when she had no clue where her dogs were—or even if they were alive.

But they still had hope they'd find them safe and sound.

Beau rushed to the shower and, after getting

dressed, ran the few errands on his list, including stopping in at the hospital. He made it to the dog training facility in an hour. The facility wasn't anything to write home about. A rectangular metal building with rolling hills behind it. A large chain-link fence covered the side and backyard. He pulled up beside Rhode, who had Air-Pods in and didn't notice him walk up to the car.

But then his window rolled down and Beau realized he'd known he was there all along.

"Dude, I thought you were slacking on the job."

"Please. I heard the sound of your motor ten miles away. Good thing you have more than one car."

Beau's weakness was fast vehicles.

"What's got you so invested…?" He glanced at Rhode's phone. He was listening to a podcast. "*Dead Talk*. Really? With Christi Cold? You know that's not her real name, don't you?"

"I know. It's Georgia Maxwell and they solved the big case she was almost killed over. Still does her podcast, though. I like it. Sue me."

"I didn't say it wasn't good. Just don't you think you need a break?"

"I love cold cases. My brain's been hardwired to solve cases since my days watching *Scooby Doo*." He laughed, but Beau heard the tinge of sorrow attached to it.

"You miss being a homicide detective?"

Rhode nodded. "I do. But I can't go back and I

can't 'if only' it because that makes things worse. I'm moving on. We just need to build the business up and I'll be fine."

"You need me to spot you—"

"I don't want your money, Beau. I just want to make an honest living and pay off the debt I owe. With no help from anyone."

Beau wasn't sure how much Rhode's debt was, but he'd run with a rich crowd a long time and he'd seen him use credit cards from the time he was nineteen. The only thing Rhode had allowed him to do was put him in rehab and it wasn't an offer from Beau so much as a demand.

"Sissy should be out soon. How was Reggie's wife holding up?" Rhode changed the subject to work and Beau shifted mental gears.

"She's not. Would you?"

"No, probably not."

"I did find a common link between the victims, though. The same photographer did their engagement photos. Saw the photo and studio credits on their engagement write-ups in the *Austin Tribune*."

The *Austin Tribune* reached all of Austin and neighboring counties.

"Good work. Does the same person at the paper do the write-ups? Because that would be a link too. Two leads."

Beau hadn't thought about that. "Probably. I'll call and ask. I want to visit the photographer.

Name's…" He scrolled through his phone, unable to remember the guy's full name. "Clem Rinehard. Works for Denford Studios out of Austin. Four other photographers on staff, but he was the one who took their photos."

"Mind taking Sissy with you?"

"No. But I can't speak for her. Where are you going?"

"Working the Henley divorce case. She's sure he's tried to kill her and that he's having an affair, but I haven't seen any evidence of it. She might be unstable. But I'll take care of it because her sister was a friend of mine."

Beau understood. He glanced at the building. "I'll go in and see how much longer Sissy will be, and you can go on and go. I'll let you know what we find out, and if she's not cool about going, I'll see what Bridge or Stone is up to."

"Bridge is available. Stone's seeing about some cattle."

Beau nodded, patted the hood of Rhode's car and jogged inside the training facility. Dogs barked and the smell of animals hit his senses. A young woman with long brown hair came into the U-shaped reception area. She wore a red polo and a soft grin. "Can I help you?"

"I'm looking for Sissy Spencer."

"You have an appointment?" she asked as she clicked a keyboard and frowned at the computer screen.

"No. We're, uh…" What exactly were they? Not colleagues. Friendship was fragile. "Friends." He went with it anyway.

"I see," she said knowingly, though she knew nothing. Beau didn't even know anything. "I'll get her." She waltzed away, but he caught her muttering, "I need Sissy's friends."

Beau shook his head and looked around the place. Down the hall, he spotted a large training area. Farther back was a glassed-in room with dozens of kennels.

"Hey, can I help you?" a man asked. He too wore a red polo with the kennel logo on it. He was tall and beefy with a boy-next-door haircut and grin. Beau guessed him to be in his late thirties. Maybe early forties.

"Someone is already. I'm here to see Sissy Spencer—we're friends."

The guy extended his muscular arm and shook Beau's hand. "Brad Fordham."

"Beau Brighton."

His blue eyes flashed recognition. "Texas oil Brightons?"

"That's us."

"And you're here to see Sissy?" His expression grew protective.

"I am. Don't believe everything a tabloid says or the media report. Lot of fake news out there." Although, the photos they'd splashed of Beau had been true. Still…they'd implied he might be a serial killer.

Brad's neck reddened. "Sorry. Just…concerned for Sissy. She's gone through a lot."

"I know. We've been friends since we were kids." He didn't like the possessiveness in Brad's voice, and a sliver of green emerged in his veins.

Brad eyed him again. "She never mentioned you."

Okay, this was turning into some kind of contest to see who had the most testosterone. Beau wasn't going to engage. "Well, even so. You own the place?"

"I do. Fifteen years now. You have a dog?"

"Not in years. I love 'em, though. Sissy's dogs are great."

Brad's eyes softened. "Did you hear they were taken?"

"I did." He wasn't going to try to out-story him. Sissy entered, also in her red polo and khaki pants. She wore her hair in a ponytail, giving her a younger appearance, not that midthirties was old. "Hey," he called, and she grinned. He'd take it. Better than the frowns she'd been tossing him over the years.

"I see you met Brad and Chastity."

The girl from the front desk waved.

"Nice to meet you." Movement caught his attention and a guy with blond hair and a wiry frame came out of the kennel with a Doberman on a leash.

He spotted their huddle and waved but guided the dog into the training area.

"That was Abe. Senior instructor, and he's way better with dogs than people," Sissy said, garnering a laugh from Brad and Chastity. Inside jokes. Beau wasn't in Sissy's inner circle anymore, which was tragic, in his opinion.

"I can wait outside, but I wanted to let you know I'm here, and no rush, but when you get a minute let's talk."

She caught his need for privacy and nodded knowingly. "Give me ten minutes to make a few phone calls and I'll be ready."

"Feel free to check out the facility, dude," Brad said. "I'd take you myself but I have paperwork."

He jerked his chin up in acknowledgment and wandered toward the back of the building. Abe worked with the Doberman and another guy. The other man had a huge protective sleeve on, and Abe was giving attack commands. The dog, following the command, rushed the guy and tore into his arm. Good thing he wore the padding or his arm would be toast. Abe called him off with another command, had him sit and gave him a treat as a reward for obeying. Abe spotted Beau and waved. "We don't really let spectators watch protective training. It can be dangerous."

Sissy entered the training area and waved off

Abe. "Beau's with me, don't worry. He won't sue if Maximus clobbers him. He has plenty of money for doctor bills." She grinned but Beau stared at the dog, uneasy.

"He won't attack me, will he?"

"Not unless Abe gives the command," Sissy said. "And Abe's not that ruthless, are you, Abe?"

Abe's neck reddened and he grinned, but he didn't answer.

"Yeah, I'm going out to the car." Beau wasn't taking any chances.

"I'm right behind you," Sissy said through laughter. "Oh, wait. I forgot my purse!"

Beau instinctively followed her to her office, which was down a hall behind the training area. Last door on the right. He glanced around. Didn't seem like Sissy at all. Not compared to her home full of warmth and color. In here, she had no photos, nothing personal except for the photo of her and Lady and Louie with their certificates for becoming emotional therapy dogs.

He didn't ask about it but remained quiet while she gathered her purse. Then he followed her into the training room, where the man was being mauled by the dog again.

Outside, Sissy halted and Beau nearly ran her over. "Beau?" she said, her voice trembling.

"What is it?" He followed her line of sight. His Audi R8's windshield and headlights had been bashed in.

Had he been followed? Had Rhode? Or did someone know Sissy's work schedule?

Time to change her routine whether she liked it or not.

SEVEN

Denford Studios was located in downtown Austin in a pretty brick building with big store windows. After calling yet another tow truck to take Beau's car, Brad had given them a ride to the Brighton ranch for yet another vehicle.

Beau had chosen a sleek gray Ford truck and mumbled something about his collection being picked off one by one. Sissy hadn't laughed. It wasn't a laughing matter, but it turned out having a fleet of vehicles had paid off, as they seemed to need one every other day.

On their ride over, Beau had filled Sissy in on the common link between victims and she'd insisted she and Rhode hadn't been followed to the training facility. Rhode would have known. However, Beau was right. She needed to change up her routine. Anyone who might have been watching her would know which days she worked and didn't.

To show up despite her protective detail was nothing short of arrogance on the killer's part.

He had some kind of invincibility complex or something.

"I don't understand," Sissy said. "Vandalizing your car doesn't hurt me, though."

"You don't feel even a little bad about my car?" Beau jested.

Sissy grinned. "I mean, what's the point? He had to know that car wasn't mine. Even if I could afford something like that, I'd never drive something so flashy."

"'Kay, now you have me feeling even worse."

"I'm not knocking your vehicle."

"No? Feels a little knocked."

She caught his smirk. Cars to Beau were like M&M's to a sweets lover like Sissy. If you dropped one, oh well. "I just don't get it."

"Maybe he wanted to make you aware that he knows where you are at all times. That you can't escape him. And maybe he wants me to know my money can't save you."

"I kind of wish I hadn't asked now." Sissy's blood turned cold. "Let's talk about something else."

Beau turned down the radio. "Okay. Stone got in touch with his old Texas Ranger friend's wife—Chelsey Holliday."

"The former FBI profiler?"

"Right. After we leave Denford Studios, we're meeting her and Rhode at a café near their Austin office."

"How many offices do they have?"

"I don't know for sure. But apparently enough for more than one location. Which is kind of scary considering their line of work," he said.

Sissy agreed. "Stone says they do threat assessments and all sorts of things that need profiles, not just serial killers." Which was good to know. "Maybe she'll have some insight as to why our guy smashed the windshield and headlights of *your* car."

"Maybe he's mad I'm investigating or that I came to your rescue and Coco's. Has to be. Beating up cars reveals rage and anger. I mean, let's count on our digits combined how many country songs have lines about cars getting keyed, kicked and crushed by jilted lovers."

"Fair observation."

Beau parallel parked in front of the studio and they entered to the smell of jasmine and someone's leftovers. Lunch had come and barely gone. Sissy's stomach growled. They were met by a receptionist, who buzzed Clem Rinehard, but were asked to wait as he was running long with a last-minute graduating senior picture.

"I hated senior pictures," Beau said. "My mom was adamant I have a billion clothes changes. It was awful."

"I loved that part. Me and a few friends got together and went on the same day. It was fun to shop for outfits, do the hair and makeup.

Of course, now I don't even want a selfie and we're in the age of photos at our fingertips." She thought of the horrific photos she'd seen of Coco and Kiefer. The video of his murder. What if this Clem Rinehard did kill them? What if he'd been trying to kill her too? Now she would be coming face-to-face with him and giving up their only secret—they were on to him for other cases besides Kiefer and Coco.

She shivered inwardly.

"Who you tellin'?" he asked, and she couldn't help but smirk again. Photos had almost gotten him in hot water a few short months ago. Beau had never been one to take selfies—sadly, she had to admit to secretly following his social media accounts—but he'd been tagged in thousands of photos taken by others.

A man who looked more like Clint Eastwood in his forties, including the squint, strode toward them. "Clem Rinehard. Y'all here for engagement photos?"

"Yeah," Beau said. "But not ours. We're looking into these couples." He handed Clem copies of the newspaper articles featuring James Beardon and Edie DuPont, Don Breckin and Babs Arlington, and Richard Buxton and Rolanda Meeks. Sissy cocked her head, noticing something on paper she hadn't in conversation. All the men, sans Kiefer, had last names starting with the letter *B*. Coincidence or was there meaning?

"Who are you again?"

"Beau Brighton, private investigator, and this is my partner, Sissy Spencer."

"Brighton. Of Brighton Oil?" he asked.

Beau tightened his lips. "Yes, sir."

Clem sized him up and grunted. "Why are you investigating these couples?"

"Do you remember them?" Beau asked, avoiding Clem's question.

"I do. Come on back to my office, where we can talk in private." He eyed the receptionist and grunted again.

His office was small and covered in glossy black-and-white portraits. "Just some of my favorites. Hard to get perfect lighting, so when you do you want to savor it." He sat behind his black Formica desk, and Beau and Sissy sat on a black leather sofa. "I have files on them. Locations for their engagement sessions. But other than that, I can't really help you. I don't know my clients personally, for the most part."

"Anything you can remember?" Beau asked as Clem turned his screen around and showed them the photos of Don Breckin and Babs Arlington, a good-looking couple in their late twenties.

"This one made the paper, I see. But here are their photos. They were outdoorsy folk, so we took it at a lake." He clicked through the photos, letting Beau and Sissy inspect them.

"Where is this?" Beau asked.

"Lower McKinney Falls."

Sissy sucked in a breath. That was where Kiefer was killed.

"The other couples have photos there too?" Beau asked.

"No." He clicked again. "What exactly are you investigating?"

The next photo was incredible. Babs splashed in the water and their golden retriever pup frolicked. Don looked on with love. The water droplets were like a rainbow over their heads. "That one is spectacular," Beau said, redirecting the conversation.

Clem smiled and glanced at Sissy but didn't say anything. Was he the killer? Did he know exactly why they were here and faking? "Thank you. I thought as much myself. It was a candid during a potty break for the pup. Best one of the bunch, to be honest. Have they gotten into trouble?"

"No," Beau finally said. "Babs was murdered."

"Oh. Oh, that's terrible." His eyes revealed surprise, but he could easily be pretending.

Beau didn't offer any more information. He'd told the truth. Left out the rest. Sissy gave him props for that. "And the other couples?"

"Sure." Clem scrolled through James Beardon and Edie DuPont's photos next. They were taken at a gazebo in a park. Not as many photos as the first couple. And lastly he clicked through

Richard Buxton and Rolanda Meeks. Their photos were done on a country-club green near the eighteenth hole. "She was the golfer." He clicked again, and they were surrounded by old classic cars in a pristine showroom. "He did something with cars. Rebuilt them maybe?"

"Mechanic."

"Yeah, that's right. But he did car shows on the side, I think."

A knock sounded and the door cracked open. A man with clear-frame glasses and hair hanging to his shoulders smiled apologetically. "Mr. Rinehard, your next session is here. And you should know the mom said the child hasn't gotten her nap. So we have that."

"Thanks, Frederick. Hold them off five more minutes if possible."

"Sure." His gaze landed on the photos, and he pushed his glasses up on his nose, then looked at Beau and Sissy before closing the door.

"Frederick has been with me almost ten years. Started out as an apprentice, but I'll be honest— I've learned quite a bit from him. He can capture the essence of a person in ways many artists dream about. Now," he said as he waved his hand, "what else can I help you with?"

Sissy had no idea. She waited on Beau to lead.

"I think that will be all." He stood and Sissy followed suit; then they left the studio.

"I want to dig into their personal lives," Beau told her once they were outside.

"I thought you already had," Sissy said as she climbed in the truck's passenger seat.

Beau started the truck. "Not the victims. Clem Rinehard *and* his protégé Frederick. Before I tip my hand, unless I already have."

Sissy buckled up. "I was thinking the same thing."

Before pulling away, Beau checked his texts. "We're meeting Chelsey Holliday and her colleague Vera Brawley at the Flavor Bean café. It's not far from here."

In about twelve minutes, they were parked and heading inside the little coffee shop, the smell of rich, nutty brew filling Sissy's senses. She used to take the Cavs to the local beanery café in Cedar Springs, and while she sipped a cappuccino, they had little doggy cookies. The owner, Lisa, was so sweet to the dogs—and to Sissy. Many coffees had been on the house after Todd died. She'd tried to pay but Lisa would have none of it.

Rhode waved to them and Sissy spotted the striking women. Both were confident in their posture, but the brunette sitting by the wall had a louder confidence than the blonde woman beside her. Sissy noticed puckers from burn wounds on the blonde's right hand and wrist.

"Chelsey Holliday," said the assertive profiler as she stood and extended a smooth hand. Sissy shook it. She'd never met Chelsey but Stone had mentioned her before when talking about his Texas Ranger friend Tack Holliday.

Vera didn't stand but extended her left hand. Sissy switched hands and shook. "Vera Brawley, very nice to make your acquaintance."

After introductions, Beau and Sissy ordered their coffees. Rhode shifted to look at Beau. "What did you find at the photographer's?"

"Not much but maybe something." He briefed him.

"Good call checking into Frederick too. You never know," Rhode said.

Chelsey tapped her index finger on the manila case file on the table. "Based on what we've read, and considering the smashed windshield and headlights on your car today, Mr. Brighton, we concur that your killer is a white male—"

"Aren't they usually?" Rhode muttered.

Chelsey smirked. "When it comes to serial killers, most often, yes. And we do think we're dealing with a serial killer. White male. Thirty-eight to forty-five. Congenial and even charismatic, able to approach the male victims without rousing suspicion. Richard Buxton and Kiefer Sterling in particular were large and pretty buff men. They wouldn't go down if they saw a fight coming, and the way the murders happened, we believe the perpetrator may be wiry or weak in stature."

Vera leaned forward. "Enough strength to over-power a woman—though he did use a Taser—but maybe not enough to take on a man fighting for his life. He's probably not stout. Scrappy but not necessarily muscular."

Chelsey consulted a few notes. "He's patient and clever. We think, because he's not assaulting the women prior to death, that his motive is based solely on the grief of the woman. She is the main target. The man is a way to get to the woman and what the killer wants—to see the grief, pain and torment."

Sissy had hoped their initial suspicions had been wrong. This was despicable.

"The photos, you said, were all close-ups. Something about him enjoys the emotional pain of women and specifically the loss of a partner."

Sissy couldn't fathom what kind of person would enjoy this kind of torture. She knew what it was like to lose a loved one. For someone to find enjoyment in that misery…it was the lowest kind of humanity, if this person could even be considered human. This was a monster.

Vera cleared her throat. "According to the notes from the female victims' families, they were each starting to heal and take steps toward moving forward with their lives. Rolanda Meeks had met someone new. Babs stopped going to support groups and even booked a cruise with friends. Edie had also met someone else. That's his trigger."

"Meeting someone new?" Sissy asked.

"Moving on. When they stop grieving, he loses that euphoria. That's why the timelines aren't consistent. Because grief looks different in many ways to each person."

Chelsey nodded, then explained further. "Once he loses it, he has one more opportunity to gain it again before he ends them. One last thrill ride. Based on the findings at Coco's—the thumb drive with the footage and the laptop—we believe his pattern will be the same with the other women too. When he tells them he has information or news about their past love, they would of course want to hear or see something. Anyone would. The video and photos he shows them are designed to return all the pain in one swelling moment. Plus extra grief at the realization it wasn't a tragic accident but murder. Cold, calculated murder," Chelsey said. "Once Coco wakens, we'll be able to confirm if this is fact."

Sissy gasped. This person was now after her. If they didn't find him and soon, she would end up a fatality too. No one could protect her from someone this vicious.

Chelsey continued, "And while we don't have definitive proof, we feel confident that during the moment that they see the truth, he takes his trophy."

"What kind of trophy?" Sissy whispered, her emotions clogging her voice.

"The last shot. The most poignant picture of grief he could capture on film. Somewhere he keeps the portrait of their faces as it dawns on them what has happened to their loved ones and what is about to happen to them. He'll have those pictures hanging somewhere or in an album of some kind. One final close-up."

"Why?" Beau asked. "Why would someone enjoy this? How can we find him?"

Vera sighed. "He's likely been riddled with loss in his life—probably at a young age and concerning parents or guardians he cared about. We're a little vague there, to be honest."

"And my dogs?"

Chelsey glanced at Vera, then at Sissy. "I can't say for sure, but he didn't steal them to scare you. He'd know that once the house burned and was inspected they'd find no evidence of the dogs. He might have a soft spot for animals." Chelsey glanced at Vera again. "Vera disagrees."

"I don't know that he's harmed your dogs, but I'm not sure the reason he took them before setting the fire was due to a soft spot but to keep you in greater anguish. If they had been burned, you'd at least have closure. By not knowing, you're staying in a state of turmoil. I believe that's his motive."

Her dogs may or may not be alive. Either way,

the killer wanted her to suffer the effects of not knowing. Sick. This man was sick.

They sat in silence for a moment, absorbing the horrific mind of this depraved individual.

"And my car?" Beau asked. "Why do damage to that? It doesn't affect Sissy. Not directly."

"He's not happy with you at all, Beau," Chelsey said. "In fact, you're very much on his radar now and in severe danger."

Watch your back.

The words echoed in Beau's head as Chelsey and Vera continued answering questions and offering as much help as they could. The profilers agreed that the two photographers at Denford Studios were good trails to run down as well as the writer of the engagement pieces in the newspaper.

If those leads failed, Beau was clueless as to what path to take. What concerned him most was how quiet Sissy had grown hearing the details of what kind of sicko had done this.

She was tough and a firecracker through and through, but even the strongest of people had a threshold before they broke. He did not want Sissy to break.

"And Coco?" Rhode asked, snapping Beau from his thoughts, his coffee now cold.

"It all depends on if she wakes," Vera said with compassion. "If she does—and we pray and hope she does—then she's a liability. She may have seen him or knows him, though he did wear the mask."

"He was in a mask, yes," Beau said, his mind replaying the image of her attacker fleeing the scene.

"He was in a mask when I saw him too," Sissy added. "And his voice was modulated. Every time."

"He's smart. Either you know him or he knows you're investigating and doesn't want you to recognize his voice if you hear him somewhere. Which means he knows there's a way for you to find him."

That felt like a sliver of hope. Finally.

But Coco was in grave danger. She was at her most vulnerable, and if the killer was as calculated as the profilers said, then he could easily murder her without anyone realizing it. "I'll get security on Coco. We've used a company here in Texas and they've done some protection detail before."

"They have a woman on staff?" Chelsey asked.

He nodded. "Two, I think. Coco's used Libby Winters before. She posed as a friend at a gala back when Coco was stalked. They found him but he received a slap on the wrist and is out."

"Could it be him?"

"I don't think so. Doesn't fit your profile. But

to be safe I'll have the security team do a check on him."

"Use the woman," Chelsey said. "Maybe she can dress like a nurse. He'll be more confident around a woman. If a man is lurking, he'll be hesitant. Not that I'm at all saying your sister should be bait, but you can catch more flies with honey, as they say."

"And a woman bodyguard makes Coco sweeter to him."

"He won't suspect. Sadly, men don't pay much attention to women as protectors unless they're in uniform. Sometimes not even then." Chelsey cocked her head. "It's not Spears and Bow Protection Services, is it?"

"It is. They're the best in Texas." His father wouldn't hire anyone but the best.

"They're actually national. Their main office is in Texas. I'm pretty sure they have one in Tennessee too. I know Axel Spears from my FBI days. Good guy. Don't know Archer Crow well, though. He's more behind-the-scenes, from what I understand. Works remotely from some reclusive cabin in the mountains."

"Rumor has it he's former CIA. Spy stuff." Rhode shrugged. "But I saw him once from a distance. He looks more Mr. Rogers than James Bond. So, if he was CIA, he wasn't the spy. He was the gadget guy. If it's even true."

Chelsey only smirked, but a spark in her eyes

seemed to give validity to the CIA rumors. Beau excused himself to make the call. He had Libby Winters in his contacts.

She answered on the second ring. "Libby Winters."

"Hey, Libby, it's Beau Brighton."

"Hey, Beau, how can I help you?" Libby asked. She was no-nonsense, to the point and direct, which he supposed in her line of work was necessary. He explained the situation.

"I'm so sorry to hear that. I'm coming off a case now, and as far as I know, I don't have anything going on but paperwork. I'll get with Axel. Also, can you send me the profile they worked up and any other pertinent information?" She gave him her email address. "I'll call you in thirty minutes. Is that enough time or do you think your sister's in immediate danger?"

Beau wasn't sure. "I think as long as she's... asleep she's okay." He couldn't say "coma" one more time.

"Okay. Give me thirty minutes. If I can't do it, my colleague Amber Rathbone can. She's flying in from a case in Seattle tonight. I know you need a female, but worst-case scenario, one of our guys can pose as a nurse. But I hear you."

"Thanks. I appreciate it." He ended the call and returned to the table. "Libby is going to call me in thirty minutes."

"We were trying to come up with any other

links," Chelsey said. "Sissy, tell us about the visit with the photographer. We want your point of view."

She pushed her drink away. "Oh. Well, he seemed nice and helpful. He showed us the photos of the couples without more curiosity than he should have shown. He remembered the couple with the dog most. Their photos were at the same park Kiefer died. Once he finished helping us, the assistant entered the room. Frederick. He seemed a little peculiar, but I know lots of peculiar people who don't commit murder."

"Wait," Beau said. "You're right. He remembered the dog couple pretty well. Remember at Rolanda Meeks's family home there were several photos in that album of her and Richard with a mixed-breed dog? Her mom said they'd rescued him and were starting their family early. What if Babs and Don also rescued their golden retriever pup from the same rescue? Dogs might be a connection."

Rhode grinned. "Dude, you are on fire. When you rescue an animal, you have to put all sorts of personal information on the adoption form. Where you live. If you have other pets and a fence. You even have to have a vet and personal references."

"So there's a good chance Lady and Louie are alive?" Sissy searched Chelsey's and Vera's faces.

"I'd say a high chance if the dogs are a connection," Vera said. "We need to know if the other couple had a dog. Did Coco and Kiefer?"

"No, but Kiefer rescued dogs and he had a German shepherd right before he and Coco got together. It passed of kidney failure."

"It's a solid lead."

After twenty minutes of more conversation, they left the Flavor Bean and headed for the car. "I'm going to call Babs's and Rolanda's families and ask a few more questions," Beau said. "And I need to find out where Kiefer rescued his German shepherd."

Beau made the calls using his Bluetooth speaker in the truck. Babs's and Rolanda's families confirmed the dogs had been rescues from Precious Paws Rescue, which was a facility located on the outskirts of Cedar Springs. After calling James Beardon's family, they found out he too had rescued a dog from the same shelter. A Boston terrier he'd named Titan.

They had another link.

They were close. Beau could taste it.

But he also tasted something a bit like impending doom.

EIGHT

Beau pulled into a gravel parking lot, survey-ing the eight vehicles there. Precious Paws Res-cue looked similar to the training facility Sissy worked at, but the building was older and smaller, and the chain-link fence sagged. On the ride over, Libby Winters from the security company had called and had been given clearance to look after Coco at the hospital. She'd be working the day shift and Amber Rathbone the night shift. He'd looked up Amber's profile, unfamiliar with her. She had been a homicide detective in Memphis, Tennessee, and joined the protection company four years ago. The thought Coco had qualified personnel looking out for her 24/7 gave Beau a measure of peace.

Inside, the heavy scent of animals and waste hit his gag reflex. They were met by a man wear-ing worn jeans with muddy paw prints on the thighs, and a smile. "What can I help you with today? Looking for a pet?"

Beau glanced at Sissy but she stood stoic, a

hint of fear in her eyes. She might be looking into the eyes of her attacker. "Yes, but not for us," he said.

"Oh, we don't adopt out pets as gifts. Sorry." His dark eyes were apologetic.

"That's not what I meant. We need information about three dogs that were rescued from this facility." Beau showed him his PI badge.

"I thought I recognized you, Mr. Brighton. I didn't know you were an investigator. I'm Tim McCloud. I manage the facility. What dogs are you inquiring about? Have they been harmed?"

"No. Nothing like that. They're in good care." Beau asked about the victims to see if the manager would remember them, but a fair amount of time had passed, so he didn't expect him to. If McCloud was the killer, Beau didn't expect him to fess up either.

"Follow me to my office and I'll search the system."

"I remember Babs," a young man said as he slipped around the corner. Had he been listening in the whole time?

"Oh, hey, Coop. These folks are here inquiring about her and her fiancé. They died."

"Where's the dog?" Coop asked.

"Family took it in and it's well cared for." Beau studied the wiry man with thick dark hair that hung over his ears. Early thirties, if he had to guess.

"Good. That's good to hear."

The man seemed more interested in the dog than the humans who'd been murdered. "Why do you remember Babs so well?"

"She was just…cool. I don't know."

Babs had been a looker.

"And I'm partial to golden retrievers. They make great therapy dogs. Really know how to make a sad person feel happy." He shrugged. "I wanted to let you know the kennels have been cleaned, Tim. Gonna exercise the big dogs now."

"Thanks, Coop."

Coop left and they entered Tim McCloud's office. "Okay. Do you know who they adopted under? His name or hers? You know what, I'll just search them all." He glanced up.

"We know the retriever was in Babs's name. And we know that James Beardon got a Boston terrier here."

"Yep. I see that."

"Richard Buxton would be next. He had a mixed-breed dog."

"Richard Buxton. Yeah, a mixed breed. Probably a shepherd/husky mix. Looks like they did all adopt from here. But other than that, I don't really know how we can help you."

Beau dreaded the next question. "One more name."

Sissy glanced at him and sucked her bottom lip into her mouth.

"Kiefer Sterling."

"Kie…fer Ster…ling," McCloud said as he typed. "No, I have no one by that name."

Beau only relaxed minimally. "Sorry, this is the last one for real. Coco Brighton."

"Co…co… Brigh…ton. Nope. Sorry. What breed did they have?"

"He had a German shepherd."

"Well," McCloud said and stood, brushing the sides of his jeans, "they didn't get him from our rescue."

So were the dogs not a link? Or maybe the fact they all owned dogs was significant to the killer? If so, how? The dogs hadn't been taken upon the crimes. They were with family members who'd taken them in.

Beau had more questions piling up than he could answer.

"Thanks for your time." Beau paused. "One other question." Beau pointed to a series of glossy black-and-white photos of a very large and gorgeous pit bull behind the owner's desk. "That your dog?"

Tim glanced up. "Yeah. That's Sheila. Named her after my late wife. They had similar personalities."

Beau wasn't sure if that was a good thing or bad thing, and Tim wasn't giving any indication he was kidding around. Pit bulls could be aggressive, but were often used as nannies for children. Maybe a bit of both. "You take the pictures?"

"I dabble in photography. Needed a hobby after Sheila died. But those were done by Coop. That's how I got into it."

Coop—the man who remembered Babs and was concerned about the dog left behind from her death. Beau's red flags flew high. "Well, they look great."

"Thanks. I enjoy the memories when I see the ole girl. But I also remember that nothing lasts forever." He shrugged and Beau wondered which Sheila he might be referring to—or maybe both.

"This is true," Sissy said. "You get any grief counseling?"

He scoffed. "No. No one can make grief go away. You deal. Talking it out is bunk. There aren't enough words to express that kind of grief and 'getting it all out' doesn't actually get it all out."

Sissy didn't bristle. "I understand."

That was it? Wasn't that the crux of what she did for a living? Helping people through their grief? She had no rebuttal? "If you can think of anything else, let us know."

"Will do."

Beau and Sissy left Tim's office. Out of earshot, Beau said, "We have a pool of suspects and that's about all. Tim, Coop, Clem Rinehard and even his assistant Frederick are all photographers—amateur and professional—with a connection to the victims. Let's see if any of them has a record. I'll text Dom."

"We should check to see if any others have suffered loss like Tim. Chelsey said that the killer might have had great loss in his past. Maybe Tim's wife's death was what Bridge calls a trigger. Setting him off on a killing spree."

"Good idea." As they headed for the car, Beau asked, "Why didn't you respond to Tim's opinion on grief counseling?"

"Not everyone attends grief counseling and they make it through fine. One can't change an opinion in five seconds of debate."

Guess that made sense.

"I didn't see any photos of his wife, though," Sissy added. "Just the dog. That was odd to me. Seemed like he missed the dog more."

Beau snorted and started the truck. "I think my dad would miss his horses more than my mom. But who knows."

Sissy's phone rang and she answered. Listening to her, he picked up on the fact she was talking to the insurance company about her house, the damages and all the details. "I see. Yes." She asked several questions. Because of the circumstances, they ruled out her having set fire to her own home for the insurance money and were going to pay out. But she didn't seem too pleased. After she hung up she sighed.

"You're not happy with the payout?" he asked.

"No, that's all fine. Part of the house can be salvaged and what can't can be rebuilt, but I don't think I want to." She rubbed her temples. "Maybe I need…want… I don't know." She waved off her thought, then bit at the corner of her thumb.

"You want a house without reminders, but you don't want to forget," he said softly.

Sissy nodded. "Something like that. I haven't been able to move on. I think that's obvious, thanks to my dazed babbling during the fire. I feel like a fraud in my job. I know what I need to do. I know it's okay to move forward and to enjoy life again—that Todd would be okay with that. Leaving the house means I'm ready for something new, which I'm not. I want to stay and rebuild to hold on to us, but I know that's not healthy either."

Beau listened as she reasoned out her feelings. Like when they were kids and could talk honestly and openly. Had they built back the friendship they'd once had before it all went to pot? He hoped so. He wanted that.

"I think a piece of Todd and Annabelle live in your heart," he told her. "Your photos weren't touched. That's a blessing. To be able to look back at your wedding album and photos of your life together. But maybe building a new house altogether, or moving into a house, would give you that push over the hump you need to move forward and still be able to look back with good memories. I don't know, Sissy. I'm not a professional."

She sat silently for so long he thought he'd said too much. "No. You're right."

That was a surprise. Before he could continue the conversation, Beau's phone rang. "It's Rhode." He touched the connection on the dash to answer. "Hey, man," Beau said, "you're on speaker."

"I found some interesting information."

Sissy listened as Rhode spoke. "The dog angle was a good one. So I revisited the families' statements and found that all three of the female victims attended grief counseling and support groups at a little church only half a mile from the place they rescued the dogs. But that's not all," Rhode said, sounding like a bad infomercial. "The support group is right next door to the funeral home where the visitation and services were held for four of the victims. We may have narrowed down our killer's hunting ground— larger funeral homes and grief counseling groups in larger cities."

They hadn't checked to see where the funerals had been or the grief counseling. This was great information. They might have a lead and she might be able to rescue Lady and Louie. It was unbearable thinking what they might be going through. Her only thin hope was that this killer might hate people, but he loved animals and her pooches were safe and well tended.

"We're actually not far away," Beau said. "We can turn around and visit the support group. Not that they're allowed to give us confidential information, but who knows. People talk. It's worth a shot. It's all we have." Beau turned to her. "Sissy, you up for it?"

"Yeah. Yeah, let's go. They might be willing to talk to me since I'm a licensed counselor."

"True," Rhode said. "Keep me posted. See you tonight." He hung up as Beau was already doing a U-turn.

"Can you remember those photos you saw? You said he took pictures of Coco going inside the church and into the funeral home. That might help us find where he was taking photos from."

"Probably his car with a telephoto lens."

"If so, maybe employees from other shops and cafés noticed him. He had to have sat there for a while. He might have bought a coffee, lunch or used the restroom."

Sissy grinned. "Beau, you really are made for this job."

"Or I just watched a lot of *Murder, She Wrote*. Thanks to our housekeeper. She loved it." He chuckled and they parked on a side street near the Austin Community Church, which was next door to Hill Country Funeral Home. Directly across the street was a deli with patio seating, and lining the block were a coffee shop and several little boutiques.

Sissy nodded toward the deli. "I'm going with that patio. It's possible he was discreet with his camera."

"Maybe," Beau said. "Let's go inside the church first."

As they entered the small church, they were met by a woman with a silver bob and clear blue eyes. "Can I help y'all?" she asked.

"Hi, I'm Sissy Spencer, a grief counselor from Cedar Springs, and I'd like to talk to you about your group."

"Okay, sure." She motioned them down a narrow hall to an office that was decorated with modern farmhouse decor. "I'm Eleanor and I run the group sessions. Can I ask why?"

Sissy introduced Beau and he shared what he could about the case, listing the names of the women who would have attended.

"Oh, yes. I remember them all. How is your sister, Mr. Brighton?"

"She's hanging in there. Time will tell."

"She'll remain in our prayers. How can I help you with the other women?" She folded her hands together in her lap and leaned back in her chair. "I can't share what they discussed."

Sissy licked her lips. "We don't need confidential information. This is more about the visits themselves. Did the women come regularly?"

"They did. Until we saw some healing, and even then, some continued. To be a part. They'd made good friendships. That's the point. Not to go through it alone, but you know this, Miss Spencer."

Miss. Sissy had never gotten used to being *Miss.* "Did they befriend any men—not necessarily romantically but friendship? Particularly the same man?"

Eleanor inhaled through her nose as she thought, her eyes focused on the ceiling. "I wouldn't single out one man. All the women were friendly, but I do remember after a group session Babs Arlington meeting a man across the street at the deli. She seemed pleased and surprised to see him. He hugged her. I didn't get a romantic vibe but it was personal. He had blondish-brown hair and was thin like a marathon runner. He wore sunglasses. They sat at the patio table and were talking when I left. I remember it because normally after group she met up with a female friend. This was the first man, and after the death of her fiancé, it meant something big."

"Did you ever notice him again or any man with either of the other victims?" Beau asked.

She clucked her tongue. "Maybe. It was winter and Edie DuPont was last to leave. It had been a particularly rough week for her. I think James had been gone about two or three months. We stepped out and it was unusually chilly. I walked across the street to my car, but she headed next door to the funeral home. A man stood in front and she hugged him. He wore a stocking cap and sunglasses, so I can't be certain it was the same person who was talking with Babs. Sorry."

So did that mean they knew their killer—or did they simply know a man who met them on a busy street? "Thank you for your time, Eleanor. If you remember seeing a man with Rolanda Meeks, please call me." She handed her the business card.

"Did the man Edie talked to come from the funeral home or was he going inside?" Beau asked.

"He was on the steps as if coming from inside."

"Do you remember that date?"

Eleanor seemed apologetic in her smile. "No. It's been so long ago, but I know it had to have been a Tuesday in February. She'd been particularly upset that Valentine's Day was coming."

That would help them narrow down a timeline. "Thank you." Sissy stood and Beau followed her outside. She let out a sigh. "I really wanted this to be a break in this case, you know?"

"I do." He stopped and stared at the funeral home. "Why would the man Edie met be in the funeral home? Could he have been stalking someone else?"

"I haven't been in a funeral home since Todd

died," Sissy said, following Beau's line of thinking. She knew he intended to visit Hill Country Funeral Home.

As she suspected, Beau laced his fingers through hers and led her inside, where she was assailed by the acute floral scent. The building was silent and eerie. Sissy never had liked funeral homes. No one did, she supposed. A thin man in his fifties exited the large visitation room where chairs had been placed in two sections. His navy suit was neatly pressed and complemented his sharp red tie. He didn't look like the funeral directors she remembered from childhood with thinning gray hair and severe parts or the director who'd been in charge of Todd's funeral.

The hallowed silence reminded her of that day she said her final goodbyes to Todd. Hushed whispers, sniffs and a few laughs from friends and family remembering Todd's humor and kindness.

She did not want to be in this place.

"Can I help you?" the man asked in a reverent tone. "I'm Jerry Johns, the funeral director."

"Yes," Beau said in a soft tone, as if they'd disturb the dead or disrupt the hanging silence. He introduced them and explained their business. "Have you seen anyone that might fit that description coming into funerals on more than one occasion?"

Jerry frowned. "I don't think so, but follow me. We can talk more privately in my office."

Beau leaned in to Sissy. "He kinda fits the profile and description, doesn't he?"

She studied Mr. Johns. He was wiry and below average height. His beard was short and neat. But she wouldn't say his hair was blondish brown. More brown. But yes, he could fit the description. He saw grief on a daily basis, and if he had some sick grief fetish, he'd have a jolly good time at this profession. The thought sickened her. "Maybe," she whispered through the side of her mouth.

Inside Mr. Johns's office, they sat opposite the desk. He worked through his computer system for funerals on those dates. "I did have a funeral on every Tuesday in the month of February, but I have no way to know if the same man attended each one. The guest books go to the families so they can send cards or have a record of who attended. It's hard for them to remember who was or wasn't there. It's a blur really. That's why we try to make things simple."

Simple. Sissy almost laughed. Dying was outrageously expensive. It nearly crushed their bank account when Dad and her sister, Paisley, died and again when Todd passed. "So, no one comes to mind who might be here for many funeral services?"

"No, I'm afraid not. Just employees, of course."

"Can I get a list of your male employees?"

"Can I ask if you have a warrant? I'm not comfortable with where this might be leading. My employees are compassionate, good people. They would not have murdered these women whose fiancés have died." His scowl matched Beau's.

Beau kept the fact the men had also been murdered close to his vest. They didn't want this leaking, and so far it had been quiet. "We don't have a warrant, but it seems like you're trying to protect someone. If they're good people, then it shouldn't matter if we know they work here."

Sissy discreetly pulled out her phone and googled the funeral home. Its website listed staff. But that probably didn't include everyone. In the online photos she didn't see anyone fitting Eleanor's description of the man Babs or Edie both saw nearby. "Where's your restroom?" she asked. Maybe someone else would give her a list if she bumped into an employee.

"Go past our first service room and make a left. Last door on your right."

She nodded and excused herself, needing a breather anyway. Being here brought up too many memories of her father, sister and Todd—and baby Annabelle. It was all too overwhelming.

She tried to keep her thoughts contained to the case. Why wouldn't Mr. Johns give them what they asked for? That seemed suspicious. Was he protecting someone? Protecting himself?

Hairs rose on her neck at a chilling awareness.

She turned as something crashed down on her head.

As she crumpled, everything blurred into blackness.

NINE

Sissy's head ached as she opened her eyes, dazed and in pitch blackness. Where was she? Her eyes wouldn't adjust. She lay on her back, something plush underneath her. Her foot was chilly. She was missing a shoe. Struggling to sit up, she bumped her head on something hard.

She was in something. Confined. As she ran her hands beside her, awareness smacked her and spiked her pulse. A scream burst from her lips.

She'd been locked inside a casket!

Frantically, she pushed on the lid, working to force it open, but it wouldn't budge. The tight space stole her breath and nearly paralyzed her in place.

Was she in a hearse about to be transported to a cemetery, buried alive?

Another wave of panic released and sent her into a screaming fit.

"Help! Let me out. Somebody help me!" Tears sprang from her eyes, rolling down her cheeks and neck. "I want out! Get me out!" Her chest constricted and nausea swept over her.

Sweat slicked her temples. It was like an oven in here, stale and heavy; her head spun with light-headedness and it dawned on her—caskets were airtight and waterproof.

Air. No air!

Forcing herself to settle down, she slowly breathed. It wouldn't take long to run out of oxygen.

How long did she have? Thirty minutes? An hour?

Beau could search that long and easily not find her. She didn't even know where she was. Her body trembled with anxiety and her head ached where she'd been hit.

If she didn't scream she might not be found, but if she did scream she'd lose what precious little oxygen she had left.

Lord, help me!

She pushed on the lid with all her strength but she was stuck.

She was going to die in this dark, locked box. Reality struck with another heavy blow. This was exactly how she'd been going through her days since she'd lost Todd and Annabelle. Alive but locked in the darkness of pain and suffering.

Unable to breathe or to see any light for the future.

Trapped.

Now. Now she wanted nothing more than to be free, to breathe, to feel light shine on her face.

The air continued to thin as the casket grew increasingly hotter. Her lungs began to tighten and her breaths came in short pants. An eerie exhaustion leached into her bones and she closed her eyes.

This was not what Todd would have wanted. He would have wanted her to finish her race well. As darkness engulfed her, a final fuzzy thought flickered.

She wasn't going to finish at all.

Beau frowned as he rushed through empty halls, scanning each room he came in contact with, but so far, he hadn't found Sissy. "Sissy," he called, hearing the panic in his voice as his heart rate spiked.

She'd left for the restroom almost thirty minutes ago. The first ten minutes she'd been gone, he and Mr. Johns carried on a conversation, but then the funeral director had excused himself. Five minutes after that, Beau thought maybe Sissy had been overwhelmed by bad memories and needed time to regroup. But then fifteen minutes passed and Mr. Johns had returned. The conversation was over and he'd left with a card and hunted her down in the bathroom. She hadn't answered his calls from outside the door. He'd gone inside to find the bathroom empty, and fear rose within him. After checking the men's room, he'd known something was wrong. She'd have never left her purse hanging on the chair in Mr. Johns's office if she hadn't planned to return.

He'd checked outside and down the street.

No sign of Sissy.

How could this happen under his nose? Racing back to Mr. Johns's office, he asked if he'd seen Sissy. Her purse was still on the chair.

The wiry man shook his head. "I'll help you find her. This is odd."

Beau wasn't sure if Jerry Johns had left the office, hurt Sissy before returning and was now playing dumb.

"Suit yourself." Beau bolted from the office, barreled down the east side of the hall this time and smacked into another guy, nearly plowing him over. "Sorry," he muttered and kept going.

"Can I help with something?" the man asked.

Beau paused. "I'm looking for a woman. Dark hair and eyes. Mexican American. Real pretty."

"No, sorry. Have you checked with our funeral director, Jerry?"

"Yeah. He's looking for her too. You are?"

"Slater Piels. Mortician. Who are you?" His dark blue eyes studied him intently.

"I'm the guy looking for the woman." He didn't have time for pleasantries. Someone could have abducted her, killed her… The scenarios had his heart racing like one of his racehorses. At the end of the hall, he approached a set of steep stairs leading down into a dark abyss.

He found a light switch on the right side of the wall and an overhead dim light flickered over the staircase. As he descended, the air grew chillier and the smell grew musty. Basement.

This was something straight out of a horror show. Silent, the light above humming. Downstairs he didn't feel a light switch right away and had no time to search for one. Besides, he knew where he was. He was in the casket storage room.

He shivered and turned on his cell phone light.

He saw a switch and flipped it up, bathing the room in light. Dozens of caskets lined the room. Rows of them actually.

He shoved his cell phone in his pocket and searched the room, but saw nothing.

Then he heard a muffled noise.

Or maybe his mind was playing tricks on him. But then he heard it again. "Sissy," he bellowed. "Is that you? Call out!"

"Beau! Beau! Beau, help me!"

Sissy. He raced down the aisles of caskets, some open and some closed, calling out for her. He couldn't find her! "Bang on the casket, Sissy. I can't find you."

Staccato beating snagged his attention two aisles over.

Beau raced to the light gray coffin, unlocked it and raised the lid. Inside lay Sissy, hair matted to her tearstained cheeks and her body trembling. She drew in a breath and bolted upright. Beau lifted her from the casket, noticing she was missing a shoe. "Oh, Sissy. I'm so sorry. I'm so sorry."

He should have never let her out of his sight. Rhode had already said to anticipate the killer everywhere and Beau had failed at his job. Failed Sissy. He spotted the blood pooling on her head where the attacker had bashed her. His own blood boiled at the killer, but also at himself.

She could have died. He'd promised to protect her and had been worried he couldn't.

He was proving he was yet again a first-place loser.

"Please forgive me. I am so sorry. I can't even apologize enough."

He gently placed her on the ground; her feet touched the floor and her knees buckled. She collapsed against him, soft sobs erupting. He caressed her hair, avoiding the wound, and kissed the top of her head. "It's all right now." But was that false hope?

"I just needed a break. Then I felt a presence and turned and I was hit on the head. I don't know where my shoe is." She sniffled through fresh tears. "My head hurts."

"You've got a goose egg but it doesn't look like it needs stitches." Beau framed her face. "I should have gone with you. Stood outside the door."

"You had no reason to think anything would

happen. I didn't either. You found me." She laid her hand on his—the one cupping her cheek. "If you hadn't…"

He could not, would not, think of that scenario. A world without Sissy Spencer would be a travesty. "Did you see a face? Hear a voice?"

"Another mask, and it happened so fast."

Beau led her upstairs and they bumped into Jerry Johns. His eyes widened and he held Sissy's shoe.

"I found this in the corner over there."

Sissy reached out and took her shoe.

"What happened?" Jerry asked. "You're bleeding."

"Someone knocked her out and appears to have dragged her to the casket storage room. Any idea who that was?"

His mouth dropped open. "Certainly not any of us."

"I want your staff names. All of them."

Jerry inhaled, then let it out, and his shoulders sank. "Let me print it out. I'm so sorry, Miss Spencer, but no one here did that to you."

Sissy burrowed farther into Beau's side and he relished the fact she found him a safe place. But it also confused him. He hadn't kept her safe at all. The bump to the noggin must have her confused.

After receiving the list and questioning the staff—all of whom saw nothing, heard nothing and did nothing—Beau led Sissy to the truck and drove her home in silence. When they pulled into the drive, a blue sedan was parked behind Sissy's mom's car.

Inside the vehicle was Brad Fordham. Beau's feathers ruffled. Something about this guy grated his nerves and needled under his skin.

"Brad," Sissy said in surprise, "what are you doing here?" She grabbed her cell phone. "Did I miss a call or something?"

Brad chuckled. "Sissy. It's all good. I just wanted to come by and check on you. You were a little spaced this morning and I know stuff has been crazy." He squinted. "And by the look of it, you're not doing so well." He pointed to her head. "What happened?"

Would she tell him of the latest attempt on her life?

"Bump to the head is all. I'm fine."

She wanted to keep it private. Understandable.

"Come on in." She headed to the front door and unlocked it. "I hope you haven't been waiting on me long."

"Just a minute or two." He glanced at Beau. "I didn't realize you'd have company."

Well, guess what, pal? She does. So, there won't be any moving in on her while I'm around.

She shrugged. "These days I always have company."

Beau arched an eyebrow. He'd ignore the fact he'd saved her bacon more than once.

He caught her flinch at her words and apology flashed in her eyes.

Beau smirked and followed her and Brad inside and toward the kitchen.

"I'll be honest, Brad. I'm not much for company right now."

"I can see that and I won't stay long. I just… I'm worried about you. Something is going on." He pointed to her head. "How did you get that?"

Sissy swiped hair from her face and went to work putting water in a kettle. "I was attacked at a funeral home this afternoon." She shuddered. "Beau found me. If he hadn't… I'd be dead right now."

Brad closed the distance between them, ignoring Beau altogether, and lightly gripped Sissy's shoulders. "Sissy, I'm so sorry." He pulled her into his arms and Sissy hugged him, but her body didn't meld into his. She didn't burrow. At that sight, Beau's ego soared and his chest swelled. Sissy had no romantic notions toward Brad.

Did she have romantic notions toward him?

Did he want her to?

She broke the embrace. "I appreciate your concern but I have good protection detail."

Brad frowned. "No offense," he said, glancing at Beau, then pointing to Sissy's head, "but that doesn't look like you've been protected all so well."

Beau felt that punch to the gut but he couldn't argue.

Sissy turned the water off and put the kettle on the stove, then peeked at Beau. He couldn't put his finger on what lingered in her eyes, but her face had softened and her easy but close-lipped smile undid him. "I've been taken good care of. What happened today was no one's fault. I blame no one. You can't either."

Brad inhaled, taking his reprimand silently. "Okay. But maybe take some personal days or something."

Sissy dropped a tea bag in a light pink mug. "This guy is trying to take everything from me, and I can't give him the satisfaction. I can do my job. It takes my mind off things. Unless you fear you're in danger and want me away. I can understand that considering he showed up at work."

Brad waved her off. "We can take care of ourselves. I worry about you is all. What actually *is* going on?"

"We can't disclose the full nature of the case," Beau said, straightening. "But Sissy has been targeted." He looked at her. "It actually might be best if you take some time off."

Sissy's lips pursed. Nope. She did not like decisions being made for her. But Beau wasn't making ultimatums. "It's not a command, Sissy. It's a suggestion," Beau said.

The way surprise lit her eyes shifted something loose inside. Had she forgotten how well they once used to know one another? They'd been emotionally connected far longer than the one night they'd physically connected, but he refused to let his mind wander back to that night out of respect for her and fear it might evoke new feelings.

"I would like to continue working," she said. "I understand I can't go alone."

"We can protect you when you're with us," Brad said. "I'll make sure me and Abe or one of us is there. He's really worried too. You know he's kinda lame at expressing himself, but he's asked about you, about what's going on and why you have a billionaire bodyguard stationed nearby."

Beau ignored the dude's lame attempt at a barb. Wasn't worth stooping to the guy's level.

He wasn't the same Beau. Again, he caught the way Sissy looked at him as if he was the only man in the room.

She turned to Brad. "I appreciate that, but I have all the protection I need." She cast her sight on Beau once more, and the flicker in her eyes undid him as it dawned… She'd forgiven him. She'd fully, wholly forgiven him and was grateful for him.

The emotion punched into his lungs and tightened. If she'd forgiven him, what did that mean? Were they truly friends again? The grace she showed was completely undeserved—just like the grace God had given him. Undeserved.

This gift meant everything and he couldn't look away from her.

"I am very grateful you're risking your own life for mine. Truly," Sissy said, her voice raspy and faint. Her dark eyes locked on his, freezing him in place. Stopping time. What was transpiring between them? Beau was unsure, but whatever it was—it was good. If Brad wasn't here, he'd bridge the gap between them and beg her to reveal the emotion behind her expression.

"So..." Brad said, jerking them from the moment.

Sissy's cheeks tinged pink. "Sorry. I'm frazzled, Brad."

Brad folded his arms over his chest. "Not sure *frazzled* is the word I'd use. Look, we need and want you at the training facility. Don't be afraid to come back." He turned to Beau. "I'm sorry about your car, and the facility will be happy to pay for the damages."

"I appreciate that," Beau said, "but insurance will cover it."

"I'm gonna head out." Brad lightly touched Sissy's shoulder. "Take care of yourself."

She nodded, then stopped him. "Hey, Brad, have we ever done any dog training for the following people—Kiefer Sterling and Coco Brighton, James Beardon and Edie DuPont, Don

Breckin and Babs Arlington, and Richard Buxton and Rolanda Meeks?"

Brad cocked his head and squinted his eyes. "Not that I recall off the top of my head, but I can check when I get back to the office and text you. What kind of dogs did they have? I'd remember them easier than people."

She grinned and told him the breeds.

"No, but I'll ask Abe when he gets back. He left not long after you today."

"Why?" Beau interjected.

"He does personal protective dog training for side money." He frowned. "You don't think Sissy's attacker is Abe, do you? That's ridiculous."

"I'm not ruling anyone out," Beau said. "Not even you."

Brad snorted and returned his attention to Sissy. "I've let Abe use the building a few times, but he has his own equipment and often uses the shop behind his house. Why are these people of interest to you—minus Coco Brighton, of course?"

"Whoever tried to kill Coco may have killed these other people," Sissy explained, "and he's now targeting me."

"I'll check first thing. Promise." Brad looked at Beau. "Keep her safe if that's the case. Seems this is a lot bigger than what we originally thought."

No, it had been big from the beginning.

"Don't relay that last bit of information," Sissy

said. "We're not revealing that to anyone." Her cheeks flushed pink.

Beau wished she'd kept that to herself, but he wasn't going to make a big deal over it. It appeared she already realized she'd said too much and regretted it.

"You have my word. I won't say a peep."

"Thanks."

Brad let himself out, and Sissy turned to Beau. "I overstepped with the information slip."

Beau bridged the distance between them. "It's fine," he murmured. There was something else he wanted to discuss. "Have you forgiven me— for the past? That look…"

Sissy raised her chin and didn't look away. "What you did wrecked me, Beau. But we drove too fast from the start. I did learn to trust again, and I don't regret meeting Todd or loving him. And the truth is, if you hadn't blown me off, I would have probably never met him—never dated or married him."

Her eyes darkened as she held his gaze. "Because you'd still be with me. We would have stayed together…got married…had kids of our own."

At her words, pain and regret stung his eyes and he swallowed hard.

A slight nod revealed she'd thought about it before. About them and their future. "I would have," she said. "I was in love with you since I was ten years old. But you never stayed with any-one—still don't—and while you might not have blown me off, you likely would have ended up breaking my heart."

"No, I wouldn't have," he blurted without thinking as words embedded inside his chest "I loved you. I regretted my actions every single day. I came to the wedding to—" He'd said too much, too fast.

Sissy squinted. "You came to the wedding to what?"

Beau couldn't look her in the eye and admit he could have ruined her best day. "It doesn't matter." The truth was, he may not have ended their relationship abruptly, but she was right. It might have ended. He probably would have left at some point. "You're actually right. I would have broken things off eventually. I was a messed-up kid. I've been a messed-up man until recently." He framed her face. "I've let my dad's words chain me from trying things, following through." Words like he was either the very best or he was nothing short of a failure and a loser. He didn't measure up to the Brighton men—specifically his father. "I let him in my head in a negative way. You know this."

She nodded.

"I've quit everything and everyone for fear of failing. And for some reason, quitting or never taking something—or someone—seriously was a defense mechanism. It's easy to say I get bored quickly or I don't care. Sometimes, that was even true. But it was never true with you. Not once. Not ever."

Beau still struggled to be free of the words his father had battered him with for so many years. Some days they were easier to shed. Some days they reared their ugly head and Beau believed them.

"The new me would never intentionally hurt you or leave you or do anything that would compromise your beliefs." Not in a million years. "The new me would love you so much better, deeper, longer…forever." What was he saying? His heart was running away with his mouth like an unbridled stallion.

Sissy blinked several times. "If only people truly had forever," she whispered. "Forever is a pipe dream. False hope. You don't think when you say 'till death do us part' that it could come before even a hint of gray hair, before life really gets going, before the children are grown with kids of their own. But then it does. Unexpectedly."

"I am so sorry for everything that's happened to you, Sissy," he whispered, his heart aching at her insurmountable loss.

"When I was in that casket, I realized how much it mimicked my life now. Todd would want me to move on and to be happy again. I know I should. I want to. I do. I want to be courageous and take a step of faith. I want to fall in love and know the joy of it again."

His pulse continued to fly. Was she about to confess something he might have wanted to hear for a million years? He said he'd follow through. He'd changed, but a pinch of doubt still gave him a measure of anxiety.

"But I'm still not sure I can. And it's not fair to give you any kind of false hope or to dare tell you to wait on me and give me time. Because what I know and what I feel simply aren't on the same page and I don't know when—or if—they ever will be. If I push myself, I'll turn you into what you don't want to be. A mistake," she whispered through watery eyes.

What he'd thought was leading to a new chance had blown up in his face. It was honest and the most real she'd been with him in a long time. He didn't want to be a mistake. At the moment, and maybe forever, Sissy Spencer had no room for him. Not even a sliver of space.

Hope deflated, but he understood and appreciated her candidness. He slid a strand of hair behind her ear, letting his fingers linger against her skin. Finally, he released his touch. "I understand," he whispered. "Why don't you get some rest? I have a few calls to make."

The biggest call? A prayer to God.

* * *

Sissy stirred, smelling a familiar scent. Her eyes opened and the room was dark. Her nap had turned into a hard, deep sleep.

Slightly disoriented and groggy, she sat up, noticing the scent was more pronounced. As her eyes adjusted, she saw movement. A shadowy figure sprang toward her, a gloved hand smothering her scream. Something hard and sharp pressed into her side. A gun? She wasn't sure.

"You ruined everything," he hissed with the same voice modulator he'd previously used. "It wasn't supposed to be this way." The grip tightened but Sissy managed to grab a glass of water from the side table. She smashed it upside the intruder's head, water running down her arm and a sharp sting pinching her palm.

Released from the tight grip, Sissy sprang from the bed and wrenched open the door, shrieking for help.

Burning pain radiated through her head as the killer gained a tight hold on her hair, ripping and tugging her inside the room. Rearing back, she headbutted him and scrambled again for the door.

"Sissy," Mama called.

"Run, Mama. Go!" Sissy screeched as her attacker slammed her body against the wall.

"I will kill you! If it has to be this way, then so be it," the terrifying voice said.

She rammed her elbow into his ribs.

"Sissy," Stone barked, and she heard her brother's heavy footfalls racing toward her.

The attacker froze for an instant and then bolted for the open bedroom window.

Stone raced into the room, gun in hand. "Window!"

She switched on the light, blinding herself as she caught the dark-clad figure fleeing into the night. When she glanced back, Stone was already gone and she heard the back door slam shut.

Sissy raced into the living room as the front door blew open and a blast of damp air seeped inside. Sissy yelped, startled, then realized it was Rhode, with Beau following him. "What's going on?" Rhode demanded. "We heard a commotion."

The door opened again and Stone stormed inside, his eyes full of fury. "The scumbag got away. Who was last to leave this house? Why wasn't the alarm set?"

A few months ago, when Emily had been the target of a vicious killer, Stone had installed a serious alarm system after the ranch had been compromised. He had been religious in setting it and everyone knew to, even Beau.

Beau's head fell back and he sighed. "I didn't set it. After Sissy fell asleep I worked on my laptop and made some calls. Rhode said I could bunk in his place above the garage. I didn't think…" His face blanched and his eyes pulsed with pain. "I could have gotten you killed, Sissy."

"You sure as sherlock could have," Stone barked. "You got a screw loose? Did Rhode teach you nothing? Basic protective-duty skills, dude. Keep the subject alive and safe. Why are you even joking around with this kind of work? You should leave it to people who aren't toying with a new hobby but care about people's welfare and justice."

Beau sucked in a breath.

"Now, *wait* a minute," Sissy said. Stone had no right to cross the line, and he was hitting Beau in the most tender area of his heart with his swift and gruff rebuke.

"Yeah, hold up, bruh," Rhode said.

"No," Beau said. "Stone's right."

"I know I am." Stone turned to Sissy. "What happened exactly?"

Sissy tried to convey a compassionate and understanding eye Beau's way, but he was taking an interest in his feet. She sighed. "I woke up and he was there. Must have gotten in through my window. I didn't realize I hadn't locked it from the other day." She'd needed some fresh air and had opened all the windows in the house to get some spring cleaning in for Mama. She must have missed her bedroom lock. "Wanna yell at me for that?"

"Yeah. I do. You have to be more careful." He thumbed toward Beau. "You should have checked the windows. All the windows. Every time."

"Why didn't *you*?" Sissy asked Stone.

Stone's jaw ticked. "Because," he said through gritted teeth, "I've been working all day and when I got home Beau was kicked back with his laptop on the couch like everything was secure. I assumed he'd done his job. I was treating him as a professional—a mistake I won't make again." Stone pinched the bridge of his nose. "Did the attacker say anything to you?"

"Yes." She repeated the attacker's words. "He was livid. Enraged."

"What does he mean by this isn't the way he wanted it to go?" Rhode asked. She noticed Beau's face was beet red and he was standing farther back now as if trying to seep into the walls and disappear.

Sissy glared at Stone. "You need to apologize to Beau. He made a mistake and so did I. We're human. We're exhausted."

Stone had never liked Beau. Her brother thought him to be spoiled, bratty, and Stone knew that he had deeply hurt Sissy. She suspected Stone knew why, but he'd never mentioned it to her. But that was no excuse for acting like a hothead.

The front door opened again and Stone drew his weapon, Rhode and Beau turned, and Sissy almost screamed again.

"Where's Mama? What's going on?" Bridge asked, approaching. "She called and said she thought someone was in the house killing Sissy. I nearly had a coronary getting here."

"Mama!" Sissy rushed to Mama's bedroom and swung open the door. She found her in the closet holding her phone. She dropped on her knees beside her, hugging her with all she had in her. "Everything and everyone are all right."

"I was so frightened. I called Stone and got no answer and the same with Rhode, so then I tried Bridge."

"It's okay now, Mama," Stone said, entering the room. "Rhode and I were chasing down a bad guy. You're safe now." He helped her to her feet and her brothers all wrapped her into one meaty hug, Sissy sandwiched between them. Her brothers meant well and Stone was a fierce protector—just a little like rawhide at times.

When they returned to the living room, Beau had vanished.

His PI badge and gun lay on the coffee table.

Stone grunted. "No surprise there. Can't take a little heat, so he's out of the kitchen."

"What heat exactly is that?" Rhode's glint toward Stone was murderous. "He's been running into fires since Coco was attacked. He's been working this case as good, if not better, as any one of us and putting his life on the line repeatedly." He folded his arms over his chest. "He made one error."

"And instead of owning it, he bailed. Typical

Brighton fashion." Stone's fiery gaze landed on Sissy with devouring force. "Not owning up to his mistakes and getting out of Dodge without a single word. Sound familiar?"

He knew. Heat bloomed in her cheeks. She thought she'd hidden what Beau had done—what they had done. But Stone had known, as she'd suspected but hoped not. Humiliation continued to burn through her.

"What is he talking about?" Rhode asked.

Bridge remained silent.

But Stone held her gaze.

"It wasn't like that," she mumbled.

"It was *exactly* like that." Stone whirled on Rhode. "I blame you for even giving him a job. You know his track record."

Rhode's jaw pulsed. "I don't know what you and Sissy are talking about. But everyone deserves a second chance, Stone. You saying you never messed up? You are so quick to judge."

Stone pointed with force at the badge and gun. "That proves my point. He quit. All because I jumped him for being a screwup. Something I'd do to any insubordinate Texas Ranger when I was in charge. You don't feel any heat, any discipline, you keep making the same rookie mistakes."

"But you threw his past in his face." Sissy was more concerned with Beau's emotional state than the flub-up. "And that's a low blow. Even for you." She stomped from the living room to her bedroom, where she changed clothes, brushed her teeth and grabbed her purse, then returned to the living room, where her brothers still bickered. "I'm going to find Beau."

"No, ma'am, you are not," Stone said.

Sissy thrust a finger in the chest of her big, bad brother. "Oh, yes, I am. Rhode can take me."

Rhode massaged the back of his neck. "On this I agree with Stone. Beau isn't answering my texts and that tells me he needs some space. Give it to him. Not everyone wants to talk it out right away, Sissy."

"He's right," Bridge added. "It'll be daylight soon. I'll make some breakfast and a pot of coffee." He headed for the kitchen but called out, "And if you go rogue, Sissy Mae Spencer, we'll chase you down, hog-tie you and force you to stay in this house." He pivoted, and while his words were rough, his eyes revealed deep brotherly love. "For now," he said softly, "let the man lick his wounds and simmer down a minute. He's a man, and he needs to process without you asking how he feels and what he's thinking and without you mothering him."

Sissy wanted to ignore him and take her chances. Stone's old-school "pick 'em up by the bootstrap" pep talk/scolding didn't work on every single human being. This went far beyond Beau being called out on a mistake—it went to the core of his insecurities. But she knew Bridge was right. "Fine."

She returned to her bedroom, locked the window and flopped on her bed, heaving a sigh. Right now she sorely missed her dogs. She needed them, the peace and comfort they offered.

Her thoughts tracked to Beau, as they so often did of late. Earlier, they had had a moment. She'd realized she had wholly forgiven Beau, and that forgiveness had lowered her guard and made a sliver of room for Beau to wiggle his way inside. She'd known it since he'd rescued her from the casket, but hadn't fully realized the extent until she felt her fierce protectiveness of him. It had proved that the part of her heart that had been reserved for Todd now held Beau. It was terrifying, electrifying and confusing all at the same time.

Being imprisoned in the casket had shaken things loose. She could no longer stay trapped in a self-made coffin. She had to get up out of that grave and live.

God would help her in the fight, but she had no clue how long it would take to battle.

She thought of the way Beau had repeatedly fought for her.

Sissy, I'd run into a thousand fires for you.

She believed it. He'd proved it time and again in just days. Beau had been gentle and chivalrous. Brave and self-sacrificing.

The old Beau wouldn't have persevered in the tough times if they'd stayed together.

But the new Beau…

He had the mettle.

Unfortunately, there was a PI badge and gun lying on the coffee table downstairs, proving he too was fighting through his past. He too was in a casket of his own making. And if he didn't break free, he'd continue to make promises in vain. Promises of following through and promises of sticking it out and not quitting. And Sissy could not wait around for him to come out of his own grave. She wasn't sure she was going to make it out of her own.

TEN

Beau sat at Coco's bedside. The doctor hadn't been by yet, but it was barely daylight. He'd relieved Amber Rathbone after her night shift of watching over his sister. Libby Winters had been updating him each day after her shift. No sign of trouble, but no sign of Coco waking either.

He held his sister's chilly hand and kissed it. "I messed up, Coke. Again. Seems that's all I do." *God, why can't I get it right?*

Coco's hair was spilled out around her thin white pillow and the tubes and lines were disheartening. When he'd gone home to shower and change, he'd seen Mom for the first time since she'd flown back.

"I almost got Sissy killed," he told Coco, hoping she could hear him. "I should have checked the alarm and set it before I left the house, but I didn't. Someone got in through her window. It would have set the alarm off had I been doing it right. But I wasn't thinking. I mean, I was. All I've been doing is thinking. About Sissy. About my future. How and who I want to spend it with. But it's a pipe dream. I won't want to fail her but I probably will. And even if I was ready to take the risk, she isn't ready to take one right now." The pain and disappointment lodged in his throat like a massive icy glacier.

"Wake up and tell me I'm being too hard on myself. Tell me to stop letting the war of the past defeat me. Tell me something, Coke. Tell me anything. Just wake up."

He laid his forehead on her hand.

"I don't deserve her," he whispered. "I broke my promise. Left it all on the table. Literally." He sighed. "I wish you'd wake up. Mom said your swelling has gone down some and the doctor is hopeful. We need you. Please wake up." He squeezed her hand and wiped his eyes with the other.

A light knock came on the door before it cracked open.

Sissy.

He didn't expect to see her. Kind of didn't want to face her. "You're not alone, are you?" Surely she hadn't run off without anyone to watch her back.

"No," she said with a fair amount of irritation. "Rhode finally said he'd bring me. He's out in the ICU waiting area drinking bad coffee and feeling sorry for people sleeping in recliners. It's nice to know he actually has a heart."

Beau found that he couldn't grin. His stomach was in knots and his head spun. "You came to see Coco. I'll go."

"No. I came to find you," she said with a measure of steel behind her lovely alto voice. She dug in her purse and pulled out his PI badge. "Brought you this. Rhode has your gun. I couldn't bring it in."

"Sissy, I'm not cut out—"

"Lies, Beau. You're good at your job. You've proven it. You have what it takes. You made a mistake. So did I. So did Stone. You take your lumps, recognize the mess-up and move on. You don't get to quit."

Sissy was right, but Beau was torn and, if he was honest, terrified of failing and even afraid of succeeding. "I don't know. I struggle."

"We all struggle, Beau. I'm struggling."

"I know."

"You made me a promise once and you broke it. You made me another promise only days ago. Do not break this one."

"I already did," he said and stood, unsure if he should close the distance between them or stay at the bedside.

"No. You needed space to deal. But what you do now matters. Don't take the gun and badge back for me. Take them back for you because you know it's what you love and are meant to do." The badge lay in her open palm.

He took four slow steps and laid his hand over it, feeling the warmth of Sissy's skin against the tips of his fingers. His other hand softly trailed her jawline. He couldn't speak. He had no words.

She held him captive with her eyes. Eyes that revealed she believed in him. She didn't hold his mistake against him; nor did she think he was a loser for laying his badge down in the first place.

His lips slowly descended, connecting with hers. Yes, she admitted to possibly being able to move forward and fall in love again. The implication that if she did it would be with him drove him here, to gently exploring her lips, feeling the hope swell and soar as she granted him permission to express himself by parting her lips and kissing him back.

Familiarity returned, but years had passed and the taste of newness swirled in his blood, leaving him heady.

Suddenly, Sissy broke the kiss and covered a hand over her lips. "I can't. I shouldn't have."

"Why?" he asked, but he already knew the answer. She wasn't ready. He hadn't made good on a promise to not quit. They were still in limbo.

"I have feelings...so many. All of them are conflicted. I'm not ready. I may never be."

"You said that before." Her kiss said the opposite.

Tears sprang to her eyes. Seemed like he was making her cry more often than not and it crushed him. He'd never wanted to make Sissy cry. But he'd been a cause of those tears far too often. "I know. The best I have in me is friendship, though. Even if part of me…part of me wants to kiss you again. Right this second."

His pulse pounded in his ears. It was what he wanted too, and if he prodded or coaxed he could have it. But he couldn't be selfish with Sissy.

Not again. Not ever.

"Then I'm sorry," he murmured.

"I am too," she said with defeat flying like a flag through her eyes.

A sound drew their attention to the bedside.

Coco's fingers moved and then her eyes flickered open.

"Get a nurse!" Beau shouted and raced to Coco's side.

Sissy bolted into action, racing from the room.

"Coke! Hey, it's okay. You're safe and in the hospital. It's okay."

Nurses and a doctor entered the room, Sissy following. "We'll need to run some tests, Mr. Brighton. You can see her in a couple of hours," the doctor said, and he and Sissy were ushered out into the hall.

He didn't mind waiting as elation filled him. "She's awake. Mom told me earlier the brain swelling had gone down and the doctor was hopeful."

Sissy smiled through tears. "I'm hopeful too."

She took his hand and held his gaze. "We're friends, yes?"

It was more than he could have hoped for a week ago. "Always." But the word sliced his heart a little, leaving a dull ache. "I need to tell Rhode. We can't let the media catch wind of this or she's in real danger. If the killer knows she's awake, he'll know she can reveal his identity."

"I was thinking the same thing." She glanced toward Coco's room. "What should we do while we wait?"

"You want to grab a coffee or something sweet to eat?" Her stress-relieving go-to.

"Yeah. Sounds like a plan." She called Rhode and told him. After she ended the call, she said, "He's going to leave if we're okay. He has some work to attend to."

Beau nodded and glanced up and saw a nurse in blue scrubs, her dark ponytail bobbing as she approached.

Libby Winters.

She was tall and athletic. Her sharp blue eyes met his. "Mr. Brighton," she said and extended her hand. "Good to see you again."

"It's Beau, and good to see you." He shook her hand, then introduced her to Sissy.

"I just heard Coco woke from the coma. You won't be able to contain the news, given who you and your family are. You don't have much time before it hits. I'll call Axel. Let him know the situation has shifted into red alert and we'll beef up security."

"Thank you." Relief flooded Beau. They were already on their game and he was thankful. "I'll make sure your team is well compensated."

"I like to get paid, Beau. But I don't do this job for the money." He caught a faint scar running across her throat and wondered if that had anything to do with her job choice.

"I know, but you deserve the pay for what you do."

She grinned and nodded once. "We're not much further on the Cavaliers, Miss Spencer. But we've covered all vet hospitals and rescues within the surrounding counties."

Sissy squinted. "I'm sorry?"

Beau's cheeks heated. "I, uh, put some extra hands to work to help find your dogs. I hope I'm not overstepping."

"I'm sorry. I didn't realize you were unaware," Libby said.

Sissy touched his upper arm. "I appreciate it and I'm not upset. It wasn't overstepping. It's what friends do for one another."

Friends. Right. Another chance to remind him there was no future between them. "Yes, it is."

"I'll be going to my post. I don't want to spend too much time talking to you in case our killer is lurking." Libby patted his shoulder and slipped away with the cart she'd been pushing as part of her cover.

Sissy looked at Beau as they turned the corner that led to the elevator. "So, you'll come back to your job? Not let Stone run you off? He meant well. He just means well terribly."

Beau chuckled, then sobered. "I will. I shouldn't have tucked tail like a coward." He led her into the waiting car. "I want Stone's approval."

"Beau, you're not going to get approval from every person you'd like it from. Doesn't happen that way. You are here to do what God put you here to do. And as long as you know you please Him, it has to be enough."

Sissy was right. As usual.

The elevator stopped and they walked out to the lobby area.

"Don't walk away again," she told him, "because you're not walking away from a job—but a calling directed by God Himself. And anyone who's ever walked away from God walks into emptiness and vanity."

He grinned. "Yes, ma'am."

As they neared the truck, a dark sedan barreled down the aisle, heading straight for Sissy, who was standing in the middle of the road.

She froze.

The driver sped up.

Beau's heart jumped into his throat.

* * *

The car was zeroed in on Sissy, but her feet were cemented to the pavement. The engine revved as the driver increased speed. She opened her mouth, but nothing came out, and then she felt herself hitting the asphalt.

Her body jarred upon impact but didn't howl in pain as she expected. Coming to her senses, she knew why. Beau had shoved her from the vehicle's path, taking the brunt of impact.

"You've been hit!"

A new fear galloped through her as the car raced into the street and away from the hospital. Beau lay on the ground, clutching his hip, and his face scrunched in pain. "Beau, how bad are you hurt?"

"I'm good," he said through a wince and groan. "He clipped my hip but it was just a graze. Still, it smarts."

Sissy sat up and touched his face, which had been scraped when it hit the pavement. He could have died trying to jump in front of a car to save her. "Can you stand?"

"Yep." He grunted. "Let me catch my breath." He sat a few moments, then stood on his feet. "I'm good. Just going to be bruised. You get a look at the driver?"

She shook her head. "The windows were tinted and it happened so fast." She lightly touched the abrasion on his cheek. "You know when I said come back to work because you're good at it? I didn't mean get yourself killed."

He reached up and took her hand. "You're worth saving, Sissy."

She swallowed hard and felt the aftereffects of his earlier kiss.

Then she thought of Todd and felt the push and pull of her emotions. She yanked her hand away and balled it in a fist. "You need medical help."

He shook his head. "I have to wonder if the driver knew we were here because we were followed or if word about Coco already leaked and he was coming by for other reasons and the timing was too perfect for him to pass up," Beau said as he hobbled toward the truck.

"I think anything is possible at this point." She sighed and they slowly made it to the truck to sit and recover a moment. Beau called Rhode and filled him in. Then he called Libby and told her what had happened and that they'd be back inside in a few minutes. She'd already called Axel and they would make sure to have someone on the floor with Coco as well as someone stationed outside doing regular sweeps.

After catching his breath, Beau finally turned to her. "You ready to go back inside?"

"Yeah."

They headed for the ICU and were met by Libby Winters. "She's awake and talking." She smiled. "That's great news. But the less great news is she can't remember much about the day she was attacked. Doc said she needs time and kicked me out." She shrugged. "I get that more than you'd think." She looked at Beau. "You see a doctor?"

"I'm fine. Really. Good work."

Libby didn't seem to believe him either, but she didn't press the issue. Beau left Sissy to speak with the doctor and find out if they could visit Coco.

"So, are you two together?" Libby asked. Well, that was nice and blunt.

"No. Why? You interested?" A tiny barb of jealousy poked at her side.

Libby snorted. "I don't date clients, colleagues or big kahunas. And he's two out of three. I just noticed the way he looks at you and protects you. It's more than the job. I've been doing this a long time, and was in the Secret Service before this. I'd lay down my life for whoever I'm hired to protect, but I don't look at any of them the way he looks at you. Mostly because I'm looking for threats." She laughed. "So I was curious, and my toxic trait is asking too many personal questions that aren't work-related or my biz."

Sissy smirked at the woman's humor and candidness. But those candid words also ate at her. How did one define what she and Beau were to one another? "We've been childhood friends and we have a history, but it's too broken for us to—"

"If two people both want to fix something, it's never too broken, Miss Spencer. I'm overstepping—again, toxic trait." Her intense blue eyes sparkled and Sissy spotted the teasing but also the truth in her words.

"Sometimes it is too broken. I'm a counselor, so I know this."

Libby shrugged. "I'm a Christ follower, so I believe that anything is possible if God is in it and two people agree to build something. But it definitely takes two. Seems he's willing."

Shame rose in her like waves of heat. "You're right," she said. "You *are* overstepping. Excuse me." She'd been rude and curt, but she didn't want to hear Libby's words because they were true. Anything was possible for God, even restored relationships.

She could not deal with another layer of truth to her sore and fearful heart, though.

She rounded the corner and Beau and a doctor parted ways. Beau's expression was grim but still ridiculously handsome. "Why the face?"

"She's awake. She's lucid and can answer questions, except she has no idea how much time has lapsed since her attack. They want to monitor her awhile more but they'll be moving her to a room later today. I just want her to be out of the woods and better."

"She will."

Anything was possible.

Those words again.

"Can we see her?"

He nodded. "He's going to let us slip in. We can't stay long, and if she becomes agitated we have to back off."

She followed Beau into Coco's room. The ventilator was gone. She was pale, and dark half-moons colored the skin below her eyes. The bruising around her neck was turning soft purple and yellow. Sissy hoped she didn't ask her for a mirror.

When they entered the room, Coco slowly turned and a smile formed as recognition lit her eyes. "Beau. Sissy." Her voice was soft and hoarse, but the fact she knew them meant everything.

Beau reached her bedside first and kissed her cheek. "Don't you ever scare me like that again. No more comas."

Her eyes filled with moisture. "I'm getting flashes of someone in my house, Beau. In black. But the face is blurry."

"His face or the eyes behind a mask?"

Coco's lips tightened. "I don't know. I just remember I was painting and someone knocked on my door and… I opened it."

Beau exchanged a glance with Sissy. "You wouldn't have opened the door to someone in a mask, Coke."

Beau was right. Coco opened the door to someone she knew. So, why was he wearing a mask when Beau had entered the house? Or was Coco confused and mistaken? Her memories weren't solid yet, and she had no idea how much time had passed. She might be thinking further back than the attack, perhaps days or even weeks.

"No, No, I wouldn't. I... It's blurry."

"Rest. It'll come to you when it does. We have leads that we're chasing down day and night." Beau smoothed her hair in a sweet gesture. He'd always doted on his little sister. Much like Sissy's brothers doted on her when they weren't jerking her chain or pranking her.

Coco gave a slight nod, then glanced between Beau and Sissy. "How long have I been in a coma?"

"Five days."

"Did y'all call a truce?"

Beau and Sissy hadn't been in a room this close together in years—minus the night Beau showed up before Christmas and watched a movie with the family. Sissy hadn't had the heart to turn him away during the holidays. But she hadn't wanted him there either. And also, deep down, she had.

Beau shifted and cleared his throat. "Yeah. We've worked through some things."

"I'm glad to hear it. I wish I remembered more. But I can't. The doctor said my memory should return, but it was traumatic, so it might be repressed. Could be days, weeks or even years. I want to remember. I want to catch this person." Her face blanched even whiter. "What will happen when he finds out I'm not dead?" Her voice trembled and she squeezed Sissy's hand.

"You talked with Libby Winters earlier, remember?" Beau asked her.

She nodded.

"Then you know you'll be safe. The whole team is taking care of you while we work tirelessly to find who did this," he assured her. "Coke, I need to ask you something. Do you remember the man who did your engagement photos?"

"Clem? Yeah. You think he did this?" Coco looked to Sissy.

"Maybe," Sissy said. "Can you remember anything about that day?"

She nodded. "I remember everything about that day." She told them she and Kiefer had met Clem and his assistant Frederick at the state park for photos. "They were kind and professional."

"Any personal conversation?"

"No... Well, I suppose. Frederick asked me several questions about being a Brighton. You know that's normal. But it's not Frederick. He's who helped get me involved with D2D."

Sissy frowned. "What's D2D?"

"Dare to Dream Dog Rescue."

Sissy felt a chill at the mention of a dog rescue. "You're helping a dog rescue charity?"

"It's a global initiative to rescue dogs out of inhumane environments. They raise money to build rescue centers, buy food and beds and equipment. All on volunteer staffing alone." She scooted up in the bed. "Why? Why does a dog rescue matter?"

"We're not sure it does," Beau said. "Go back to the night you were attacked."

"I can't remember anything other than hearing a knock and letting someone inside."

Which meant she didn't remember that Kiefer had been viciously murdered. She still thought his death was accidental. Telling her would add severe stress. Not telling her the truth felt like keeping a dark secret. But her recovery and health were the main priority. Coco was going to have to endure the horrific news all over again. Sissy's heart broke at the unfairness. She caught Beau's eyes and her gaze let him know not to go further with the conversation.

"What is going on?" Coco demanded.

"We think whoever hurt you is a dog lover. And we believe this person has also killed other women," Beau said with caution. "We connected your attack with other women's attacks and discovered that you all had the same photographer for your engagement photos. That's why we're asking about Clem and Frederick." Beau sat on the edge of her bed and waited for her to process the information.

"I see," she whispered. "I reached out to Frederick a couple of months after our photo shoot. He was very helpful and we met a few times for lunch. Then Kiefer died and I needed time. He understood, but he would check in on me from time to time."

"Yet he didn't mention any of this to us when we talked to him," Beau said, and fury fumed in his eyes. "I want Dom to bring him in. Question him."

Sissy agreed. They might have their killer. Finally.

ELEVEN

Beau's frustration tightened his neck and shoulders. Frederick Slattery hadn't shown up to work today—called in sick. At his home, his car hadn't been under the carport and no one had answered the door when Beau and Rhode had banged on it. Sissy had insisted on going along, with the promise to remain in the car. If the killer was Frederick, Beau knew she wanted in that house to rescue her dogs.

Unfortunately, Frederick was in the wind. But he'd blow back around soon enough.

Beau had combed over the staff photos at the funeral home—again—and only the funeral director, Jerry Johns, fit the description. After further digging, there were no signs Mr. Johns owned a dog or had been part of a dog shelter or rescue group. Beau was certain dogs were the key factor here. Tim McCloud, owner of Precious Paws Rescue on the outskirts of Cedar Springs, continued to be a viable suspect. Three of the four couples had adopted dogs from his rescue. What if he was lying about Kiefer? What if Kiefer had adopted a dog from him but Tim realized Beau was on to him, so he pretended he had no record? Beau was fairly certain his hunch wouldn't garner a warrant.

He now sat across from Sissy in the hospital cafeteria with a muffin and a cup of decent coffee, though he needed straight beans to munch on if he was going to overcome the exhaustion in his bones. Rhode had spoken with Coco before driving into Austin to discuss protection details with Axel Spears and Archer Crow. He then planned to take another crack at Tim McCloud, along with the other employees.

"I'm wondering…"

"Yeah?" Beau asked, not loving the flicker of an idea in Sissy's head. Nothing good was going to come from "I'm wondering."

"The CSPD can't waltz into Frederick's house without probable cause, but I'm a civilian. If I suspect he stole my dogs and I break in and find them, then that could stick. Right?"

Beau scratched his temple. "It's tricky. The laws and rules that would exclude evidence are based on protecting the citizen from the state actors, not from other citizens. So, it might stick. But if you trespass and find no dogs or evidence of crimes, you're the only one who broke the law."

"But if I find nothing, then I say nothing and

no one is the wiser." She picked a walnut off her banana muffin and popped it in her mouth. "I have probable cause. I'm desperate and Rhode says the perks of doing this job now is he's not obligated to all the rules the law is."

"Basic law he has to follow. He can't break and enter." That Sissy was even considering something illegal and dangerous proved she was at her tipping point, but he understood. Every day her dogs stayed missing was another day to slowly unravel.

"But I know he has." She tossed him the don't-argue-with-me look.

Okay, fair enough.

"I can sit here and pretend to like this muffin or I can be proactive in finding my dogs. Frederick fits. I just want to snoop outside the house."

"And if you find nothing? You gonna bust into every suspect's home, hunting for the dogs?"

She lifted her chin and he saw the defiance in her espresso eyes. "If I have to."

"And who's going to take you? Be the accessory?"

She cocked her head and smiled in a way that made him want to move every mountain in her pathway. "Why, you are." She then batted her eyelashes.

Beau chuckled at her antics, but if he denied her this, she'd find a way to do it on her own. He'd known Sissy all his life. "Lady friends shouldn't use their womanly ways to get their male buddies to commit crimes."

"Ha. Tell that to Bonnie and Clyde." She stood. "Let's get on with it."

Reluctantly, he followed her to the truck, being extra cautious in the parking lot. As they neared the vehicle, a dark SUV came around the corner and slowed. Beau gently but quickly glided Sissy behind him and laid his hand on the gun at his hip as it approached. He was taking zero chances.

The window of the SUV rolled down and a man spoke. "Easy, Mr. Brighton. Keep your weapon secured. I'm Axel Spears." The SUV fully stopped and Beau looked in at the hulking man whose biceps nearly broke free from the light blue dress shirt he wore. His blue-black hair was close-cropped and his eyes were like steel, including the color. "Just making rounds."

"I appreciate that. Thank you for all you're doing," Beau said.

"No problem. Y'all take care. We'll check in with you later." His slight drawl wasn't quite Texan. Sounded more Alabama, Mississippi or Georgia.

Axel waited for them to enter the vehicle and pull out of the lot before he moved on.

Sissy unzipped her purse and retrieved a stick of gum. "He's intense. I wouldn't want to make him angry."

"Hulk smash," Beau said, using the Hulk's verbiage, through a chuckle.

"Right?" She let out a shaky breath.

"You sure you want to do this?" Beau asked.

"Yes. One hundred percent."

Then they would.

Twenty minutes later, they circled Frederick's block, casing the house. No car under the carport. Beau parked down the road and they strode cautiously up the sidewalk to the house.

Beau knocked. If Frederick was home, they'd simply question him again.

No one answered. Sissy peered in the window, trying to find signs of him through the crevices in the blinds. "Doesn't seem to be home."

"Then let's find a way in without destroying property. Less charges, the better," he muttered as they poked around the house, keeping an eye out for people passing by or neighbors.

"Beau!" Sissy whisper-shouted. "This window is open."

The window on the west side slid open into a spacious living room. Trees edging the property lines supplied their cover. Sissy started to climb inside, but he stopped her. "Wait. I'll go."

"You can't."

"I can if you can." He slipped on latex gloves, then handed Sissy a pair. "For good measure." He climbed inside and helped Sissy in. The house was dark and smelled of a recently cooked meal and Old Spice. It wasn't a large home, but it wasn't a tiny house either. A fifties-style brick home in an older neighborhood. "Let's stick together."

Sissy nodded and they looked around the living room, then moved to the kitchen. Sissy called out, "Lady. Louie." If they were here, they'd know her voice and they'd bark. But there was zero noise except the hum of the refrigerator and the clatter of ice dropping into the freezer bucket. A kennel, big enough for one large dog or two little ones, was stationed by the back door with water and food bowls. But no dog.

Sissy knelt and studied the inside dog bed. "White hairs, Beau. It could be from my babies." Hope and fear registered in her voice.

They finally made their way into the primary bedroom. Frederick was a bed maker and his room was tidy. Lining the walls were glossy black-and-white portraits of a large Belgian Malinois and a Great Pyrenees. "The white hairs could be the Pyrenees, Sissy."

Sissy continued studying the photos.

Beau opened and closed dresser drawers.

"I don't think my dogs are in there. What are you looking for?" Sissy asked and opened the closet.

"More thumb drives or scrapbooks. I bet he has a dark room. Glossy black-and-white photos like that aren't done digitally."

"Maybe," she said absently and entered the closet. He heard her rummaging around. Then she called out, "Beau!"

Beau closed the top drawer full of mismatched socks and rushed to the closet. Sissy held up a photo and Beau's mouth dropped open. "What in the world?"

Sissy pointed to a small shoebox. "This box was solid white. It didn't fit with the other shoeboxes."

Inside the closet were several shoeboxes stacked neatly, all legit name-brand shoes. He opened a few. All shoes matched the box descriptions.

"Good eye, Sissy."

She carried the white shoebox to the bed, then opened it. Beau stared, stunned. Dozens of photos of Coco lay inside. "We've got him," Beau said. "We have him now."

Sissy frowned. "You said she'd been feeling watched, right?"

He nodded.

"Now we know she was."

Beau's stomach dived. "We need to call Dom. Now."

And find Frederick.

TWELVE

Sissy wasn't sure what would happen now. She could technically be arrested for trespassing and breaking and entering. But it was worth facing charges to find the killer and maybe the judge would go easy on her if she did.

They stood in the kitchen, Sissy inspecting the kennel more thoroughly, trying to distinguish the white hairs. Could they be Lady's and Louie's? Beau had the phone to his ear, but Dom's very loud and angry voice penetrated the line. Words like: "How stupid can you be, Brighton?" Beau's jaw was set and his eyes steely. Would he run at the verbal bashing or would he stick it out? Right now, Sissy had no time to ponder what Beau might do. But if they left and Frederick had any idea they'd been here, he might destroy the evidence. She raced back to the bedroom to snap a few photos for proof.

Beau entered the room. "So…" he drew out. "Dom's not happy about the situation. He's in a predicament with the fact you and I broke into a guy's house. He's looking into Frederick's history and hoping he can find any charges or restraining orders to prove a pattern of stalking. If he can, with the dog hair and Frederick's ties to Coco, he feels he can secure a warrant. But he's irritated. To say the least."

"Well, didn't he already look into Frederick? Wouldn't he already know if he had a restraining order or charges?"

"Maybe. Depends. Come on. Let's get out of here."

She nodded and followed him from the bedroom, but as they entered the hall leading to the living room, a low growl sent Sissy's hairs to attention on her neck. A large Belgian Malinois bared its teeth, its hackles raised.

"Easy, boy," Beau said.

Frederick entered the hallway and startled, then shouted, *"Toten!"* The muscled dog sprang toward Beau.

"Get in the bedroom. Go!" Beau shouted as he grabbed a framed picture from the wall and used it as a shield.

Sissy ran for the bedroom and headed to the window. She was halfway through it when Frederick clutched her legs and dragged her inside. "What is that?" he hollered and pointed to the shoebox on the bed. She hadn't put it back! "What have you done?" He tackled her to the floor.

"Where are my dogs?" she returned as he

rolled her over. She bucked and swung, clipping him in the jaw. Outside she heard Beau shouting and the dog snarling and growling.

Grabbing a heavy crystal tray that held loose change from the dresser, she whacked Frederick in the head with all her strength. Change clattered to the carpet and he slumped with a trickle of blood running down his temple. Her stomach roiled at the sight. Had she killed him? The idea sent a wave of panic through her and she checked his pulse with trembling fingers.

Alive. But out cold.

She rushed to the hall to see that Beau had managed to fend off the dog with the framed picture but the Malinois was eating its way through it.

Toten. Meaning *kill* in German. Frederick had trained the dog like Brad and Abe. With foreign-word commands so attackers couldn't use it against the owner.

"Mach sitz!" Sissy commanded with authority. The dog paused, looked at her. "I said *mach sitz.*" She snapped and held up her index finger.

The dog immediately sat quietly, leaving a huffing and puffing Beau on the floor, chest heaving.

"Platz!" she called, and he trotted into the kitchen and into his place—the kennel. She closed the door and latched it. "Good boy," she

said. The attack on Beau wasn't this poor dog's fault. He was obeying orders. Rotten orders.

"Nicely done," Beau said as he pointed toward the bedroom. "I've called Dom instead of 911. Let's hope we get a pass." He bent over at the knees and Sissy noticed bleeding scrapes and bites on his arm.

"How bad are they?"

"Not stitch-worthy. When the glass on the frame broke, it slowed him down. Is he hurt?"

Sissy studied the dog, lying sweetly in his kennel.

"Seems okay."

"Where is Frederick?"

"I hit him in the head and knocked him out, but I don't know for how long."

Beau ran into the bedroom where Frederick lay motionless.

Sissy sidled up beside Beau and wrapped her arms around his waist. "We got proof. No dogs, but proof." Maybe this was all over.

"Thank you for saving my life. Was that German you spoke?"

She nodded against his chest, feeling his heart race. "This could have ended way worse." Like the both of them dead.

A car door slammed. Sissy ran to the living room and peeped out the window as Dom marched up the sidewalk to the front door. Still in gloves, Sissy opened it.

"This is by far the dumbest mess you've gotten yourself into." Dom strode inside and into the bedroom where a passed-out Frederick was starting to rouse. Dom shook his head. "If I wasn't a man of integrity I'd let you off and make something up, but you'll be happy to know the fact he has a restraining order in New Mexico helps your cause tremendously. I'll need a statement from you. Frederick may or may not press charges. Due to mitigating circumstances and if he turns out to be your attacker, you should be okay."

"I understand," Sissy said. "I broke the law. But look." She pointed to the shoebox on the bed and the photos splayed on the bedspread. As Dom surveyed the photos, she added, "And he tried to kill me!"

"You broke into his house. It's called the castle doctrine, or as you might know it—and ignored—the stand-your-ground law," her cousin told her. "You've really made a mess here."

Dom was right. Any homeowner would have tackled an intruder in their home—or called the cops. Sissy had been in the wrong.

Dom pointed to Beau's bloody hand. "What happened there?"

"Dog attacked me."

"If you hadn't been in the house, you wouldn't have been in that situation." Dom frowned, his lips turning south.

"You sound exactly like Stone," Sissy said with an eye roll.

"Stone is a smart man." He glanced at Beau and the implication landed.

"This was my idea. Not Beau's. He didn't want me to, but I was doing it either way." She folded her arms in a stubborn stance.

Frederick moaned.

"Well, sleepyhead is waking. You two go on. I'll handle it from here." Dom retrieved handcuffs as he muttered under his breath. She hoped she hadn't gotten her cousin in trouble too.

Beau laced his hand in hers and squeezed as they walked down the sidewalk to the truck. "Let's get you home. But until we know for certain that Frederick is the man after you, I'm assuming nothing."

But this had to be the guy. Maybe he'd tell Dom where her dogs were. It wasn't fully over until she had her babies back safe and sound. She climbed inside the truck. "I understand." Her phone rang. "It's Abe." She answered. "Hello."

"Hey, what's up?"

"Nothing. Nothing I want to talk about, anyway. What's up with you?"

"Trying to get Mr. Hank's Doberman trained. Brad wanted me to call and let you know that you have some certificates to sign before tomorrow's graduation ceremony. Can you swing by?"

She'd forgotten all about that. Guard dogs,

working dogs and therapy dogs were graduating. "Yeah. No problem. Give me about thirty minutes."

"No worries. You any closer to figuring out who's been coming after you? And why?"

"We have someone in custody."

"Really?" he asked with a fair amount of surprise.

"Yep."

"Well, good. See you in thirty." Abe ended the call.

"Can you drop me off at the facility?" she asked Beau. "It won't take too long. You can wait in the car and make phone calls or something. I need to sign graduation certificates for the dogs and their handlers."

"Sure."

"You think it's over?"

"It's not over until it is."

That was what scared her.

What if it wasn't over?

Sissy opened the truck door at the dog training facility. "You really don't have to stay. I can have Brad or Abe bring me home."

"I want to call the hospital and check on Coco. Mom sent me a text an hour ago that she's there and my dad flies in tonight."

"That'll be good. Maybe you'll have hopeful news to share with him. Not that it matters if he approves, but good news can sometimes soften blows and bring reconciliation."

"I know."

"Back there when Dom chewed you up on the phone…it was nice to see you stand strong and not run."

He held her gaze and resolve steeled his eyes. "I told you I'm done running. I mean it this time."

Sissy hoped he meant every word.

Beau's phone alerted him of an incoming text. "It's Rhode. He's at the station with Dom and they're about to interview Frederick Slattery. They found another kennel in his storage shed out back and… Lady's pink leash was inside. He wants to know if I want to be there for questioning."

An olive branch that would build Beau's confidence that he was an equal, a professional. "We've got our guy, don't we?" Hope rose in her chest, but she reminded herself that finding the leash didn't mean they'd locate the dogs. "Go. Find out where he has my dogs. I know they're alive. I feel it and he's a dog lover. He wouldn't harm them. Chelsey was right about him being soft for dogs."

"You sure?"

Sissy grinned. "I'm safe. Make him tell you where my babies are. By any force necessary. Even waterboarding."

Beau chuckled at her joke, but she wasn't 100

percent kidding. She'd already crossed all kinds of lines to get her fur babies. "We'll get him to talk. Without that."

She laid a hand on his shoulder. "I'm glad we're friends again, Beau. I've been so mad, but I've also missed you." She hurried inside, slightly regretting her words of missing him, but it was true. She hadn't missed him while she was married, but lately so many fond memories had surfaced. Their friendship and easy banter. Before it had gotten out of hand it had been a real, genuine friendship.

Inside, the facility was empty. "Brad? Abe?" she called. Nothing. They might be training dogs outside. She glanced in rooms as she breezed by, but neither was anywhere to be found, not even in the indoor training area. A few pieces of training equipment were out, so someone had been in here recently. She strode down the long hall toward Brad's office, the flickering light overhead signaling a ballast was out. Brad wasn't in his office. An eerie sensation fluttered across her skin, chills scraping her spine. She peeped into Abe's office and it was empty as well.

A couple of barks from the dogs in the kennel echoed in the space. Sissy noticed an old junk closet that was usually kept locked was cracked open. Maybe Brad was cleaning it out. "Hey," she called and approached the closet.

She switched on the light and curled her lip at

the mess. Old equipment, kennels, boxes were piled on each other. One box caught her eye. A simple white shoebox like the one they'd found at Frederick Slattery's home earlier. She wiggled through the mounds of old junk, batting cobwebs and sneezing at the dust. Finally she knelt and grabbed the shoebox. Lifting the lid, she gasped.

"You shouldn't be in here." Abe's voice startled her and she turned, distracted from the contents in the box.

"Abe. Where's Brad?" Ice ran through her veins. Was Brad even at the center? Had Abe lured her here? Were these photographs he'd taken? Of the victims, including Kiefer and Coco.

"Brad doesn't let us in here."

"But you have a key." She'd seen him come in and out of the closet before. She slowly stood and he eyed the box. Abe did private dog training. He'd been asking about her and the case. Brad said so. Her hands trembled and she realized she was trapped. There was no way to get out the door without bypassing Abe. She scanned the room for anything she could use as a weapon. "Back up and let me out of here."

"What's the matter with you?" His eyes narrowed.

"Did you take these pictures? Did you…did you kill all these people?"

Abe inched toward her. "Just breathe. You're talking out of your head."

A pop sounded and Abe's eyes widened. A tiny spot of red emerged through the front of his shirt and spread quickly.

Abe collapsed.

Sissy stood stunned, gaping at Abe's lifeless body and then up at the shooter.

At the police station, Beau stood with Rhode behind the glass as Dom sat across from Frederick Slattery in the interrogation room. The suspect's hair was mussed, his eyes were glazed, and his knee bobbed like a cork in the water.

"Easy question," Dom said. "Why do you have photos of Coco Brighton?"

Frederick's hands were laced in a ball on the table, his thumb furiously rubbing the outer edge of his index finger. "I don't know. I didn't take them."

"Yeah, you do. She's pretty, beautiful really. She's walking art. A man can't blame ya for being drawn by that and wanting to capture her into a photo. They're great, man. You have real talent. I can see why you'd want more of them. Become a little transfixed on her." He shrugged as if he related completely with Frederick.

Beau saw the detective's technique. Be on the suspect's side, gain his trust. "Dom's really good. He'll get him to talk." Beau hoped so, anyway.

In the interrogation room, Frederick met Dom's eyes and studied him. "I didn't take those photos.

I don't know how they got into my house. All I know is the two people who were asking questions about Clem's clients were inside my house when I got home. I didn't know what to think and I sent Rufus—my dog—into attack mode. I was defending myself and my home. It's my right."

"They're dusting those photos for fingerprints now. Are you saying we won't find yours?"

Fredcrick's face reddened. "That's what I'm saying. Look, I know Coco. She wanted to be involved with the dog rescue. She's a great lady, but I never took any photos except the ones for the dog website. Look for yourself."

Dom nodded.

Beau sighed. "He sounds convincing."

"I agree and he's not revealing tells of someone lying." Rhode frowned. "If he's telling the truth…"

"Then someone knows he had a connection to Coco and is framing him. Someone who might know that Frederick could be connected to the other couples too." Beau's stomach knotted and he texted Sissy. You done? I can leave now.

No response.

"And if that's true," Beau added, "then Sissy shouldn't be left alone. I'm heading to the training facility. I'll call you when I have her."

Rhode gave him a thumbs-up and Beau hurried to his truck, hopped in and drove to the facility. He called again through his Bluetooth speakers, but the calls continued to go straight to voice mail.

Beau never should have left her there alone.

He whipped into the parking lot and turned off the ignition, storming inside the building. "Sissy!" he called and checked rooms and other offices as he made his way to her office. Her phone sat on her desk with her purse. So, she was here.

Relief flooded his senses and he let out the breath he'd been holding. When he found her, he was going to give her the business about not having her phone on her. He left her office and made his way outside, but she wasn't in the fenced-in yard.

In fact, the place was empty.

He went back inside the indoor training arena and searched, followed the hall, opening and closing doors, hunting for her. A prickling sensation skittered across his skin.

An office door was open but no one was inside. "Sissy," he called again.

Nothing.

Down from the office was another closed door. He turned the knob but it was locked. A warning rang in his gut and as he glanced down he noticed a pool of red oozing from underneath the door. His head turned fuzzy and his stomach clenched so tight he nearly doubled over.

Blood.

THIRTEEN

Sissy rolled around in the darkness, unable to see or wriggle free from inside the trunk. Though bigger than a casket, it still made her feel like she was enclosed in a death tomb.

After Abe's murder, she'd fought with the shooter, but she'd been Tasered and tied up, then marched out the back door at gunpoint and forced into the trunk. She'd begged and pleaded, but it had fallen on deaf ears. Sissy's pulse pounded and she couldn't process...couldn't understand. They'd been wrong.

All of them.

Including the profilers. They'd been right about all of it except one thing. They'd assumed it was a man.

Crunching gravel sounded as they bumped along and the car stopped. A door opened and closed. The trunk then opened and the light blinded Sissy. The trunk had been so dark.

Chastity stood before her, no longer looking at her like the friend Sissy assumed she had been.

They'd worked together for years. How could she? How did Sissy not see it? Betrayal smacked her like a bag of concrete blocks. They'd had lunch many times after Todd died. While Sissy thought she was being supported by a girlfriend, she was actually giving Chastity a show.

"I thought you were my friend," Sissy squeaked. "I don't understand. This makes no sense."

"It makes perfect sense," Chastity said. "Now, get out of the car or I'll put a bullet through your head. You've ruined everything. But I'm not done yet. I get one last laugh."

"My hands are bound behind my back. I can't get out."

Chastity huffed and helped her from the trunk, not being gentle about it either. She pointed the gun on Sissy.

"Where are we?" Sissy asked. She couldn't gauge how long she'd been in the vehicle or what direction they'd traveled. Nestled into the hills and surrounded by woods was a small cabin with a sagging front porch.

Leaves from the fall still carpeted the spongy earth and the wind blew lightly through the newly budding trees.

"You don't need to worry about that." Her voice was cool and full of scorn.

No wonder Chastity had used a voice modulator. She'd had to hide that she was a woman.

For a female, she was tall at five-ten and she was strong and athletic from hiking and rock climbing and running. She easily could have passed for a man who was average height and wiry.

She knew she couldn't overpower a man, so she'd made those murders look like accidents and she'd had easy access to the women. Women rarely saw other women as threats. All she needed was a Taser to stun them and she could kill them. But why?

"Where are my dogs?"

"I think you have more important things to be thinking about than your dogs." Chastity kept the gun in her back as they climbed the steps to the cabin's porch. She unlocked the door.

"You plan to kill me. Why should I care about anything else? Please make sure my dogs are returned to my family." Unless she could find a way to fight her way out, Sissy was going to die like all those other women. Tears leaked from her eyes, betraying her false bravado. But why her? Was this revenge for messing up the plans with Coco? She'd noticed the way Chastity had looked at Beau at the facility the day he'd come for her. She'd even mentioned to Sissy how handsome he was. Sissy had admitted he was and that they had a history but there wasn't anything else happening between them.

"Lady and Louie are fine." Chastity opened the door and motioned for her to enter. "And they'll continue to be. You think I'd hurt a dog? I made sure they were kenneled and in my truck before torching your house. Oh, the look on your face was priceless. And I captured it to remember over and over."

Chelsey and Vera had been right. The killer had been there watching and documenting the grief and torment.

The cabin revealed an open floor plan. Small kitchen, dining and living area and a set of stairs leading up to where she figured the bedrooms were.

"I don't understand. We found photos in Frederick Slattery's home."

"Good old Freddy. We took a few photography classes together and discovered we had a love of dogs in common. I knew he'd been connected to Coco and I also knew he had a restraining order on him for being overzealous with a former girl-friend. He was easy to frame with the photos and placing Lady's leash in his shed, and if he didn't pan out, I'd planned to frame Brad." Her grin revealed her pride. "You know, Abe isn't the only one who trained dogs on the side. I just never told anyone."

She forced Sissy to the dining area and made her sit in the chair. Grabbing ropes from the old wooden table, she tied Sissy securely.

Sissy was a therapist. Maybe she could take what she knew from the profile given—which would have been spot-on had it not been for the gender. But Sissy, like the others, never suspected it to be a woman. That was her oversight, believing a woman couldn't be so cruel and evil.

Right now, she had no phone. No way to communicate to anyone. "Beau is going to come looking for me. My brothers will and you know their law enforcement backgrounds. They'll find Abe. They'll find Brad and know you're missing."

Chastity slapped her across the cheek, the sting like wasps. "You think you're so smart. You're not. They'll question Brad—who has more photos under the crawl space in his house, and they'll find them. And if they let him go, I'll be long gone and they won't find me. And you won't be able to tell, because you'll be dead."

Panic welled in her chest, constricting her lungs and threatening a full-on anxiety attack.

Breathe.

"You're right." *Pacify her and let her know she is in control and I am not. I am beneath her.* "There is so much I don't know or understand. Help me. Explain it so I can. Have you lost someone dear? Is that what led to this?"

Chastity snorted and scowled. "Sissy, spare me the therapy diatribe."

"I just want to understand."

Chastity's smile turned wicked. She went to the dining area and retrieved a laptop, then opened it and clicked on a file. "I'm about to show you more than you ever imagined."

She didn't want to see the other victims' photos and videos. She couldn't bear it. But she'd asked to understand, and if this kept time ticking and her alive, she'd endure and hope that Beau and her brothers could and would find her.

"You think you simply interrupted my plans with Coco?" Chastity cocked her head. "Oh, poor Sissy. You've been messing with my plans for far longer than a week. You were never supposed to be in the car with Todd when the tire blew."

Sissy's blood froze and it sounded like cotton in her ears. Was she saying...? The file opened and she watched as she had with Coco's photos. Only these were of her and Todd. She watched in horror as it all clicked into place.

Todd's death was no accident.

Sissy hadn't been killed yet because she hadn't come out of the grieving stage. All this time, Chastity had taken her photos. They flashed on-screen. At the funeral. The grave site. Alone in her room, sobbing. Tons of them over the past years.

"The tire was supposed to blow and wreck him off that ravine. I knew it would be fatal. I didn't know you were going to be in the car with him until I followed at a distance and realized you were inside. I wasn't sure what I was going to do."

Chastity had targeted her long ago.

Tears rolled down Sissy's cheeks in streams. She couldn't help it. Her husband had been murdered.

"But I passed out."

Chastity snickered. "Is that what you think?"

Her blood ran cold. "Wasn't that what happened?"

Chastity showed her another photo. "You were dazed. Totally out of it. I just gave you a light knock and you went to sleep. Let me show you something."

"No." She hadn't passed out. She'd been knocked out and so confused she'd assumed that blow to the head came from the disorienting crash. But Chastity had been there. Documenting.

"It's just a video."

"No!" She would not look at her late husband's murder at the hands of a woman she'd trusted and considered a friend. "You can't make me watch." She closed her eyes. "Kill me now. I will never watch it."

"Fine," she said nonchalantly. "You can listen, then. Can't plug your ears tight enough to not hear his pleas for help and to not harm you."

Sissy began to cry. Todd. Even at the end he wanted her to be safe. To be spared.

"But know this one thing. I had nothing to do with the loss of your child."

"You slashed a tire and it blew! It's all your fault," she screamed.

Chastity gripped her chin and squeezed until Sissy saw spots. "You weren't supposed to be in that car! And I wasn't ready for you to fall in love again and move on. I've had such a great time watching you. I thought maybe I wouldn't even have to kill you. You'd grieve for the rest of your life. Like Todd deserved. But no. And to fall for Beau Brighton. You're better than that, Sissy."

Sissy sniffed. "I am not in love with Beau."

"You're a liar. I saw it when he came to see you at the facility. I knew then something had changed. You don't believe me? Let me show you." She held out her phone and Sissy couldn't help but look as Chastity scrolled through photos of them laughing, almost kissing and the actual kiss. Chastity had captured that. She'd gotten past the bodyguards to take the photo because the bodyguards were told they were looking for a man.

Sissy couldn't look away. There was no denying Chastity's claims.

She was happy. Again. She was in love. With Beau.

"Todd would have wanted me to move on."

"No. He wouldn't have. They never do." Chastity spit on the floor in disgust. "My mom and I were never close. Not until my dad died. In her grief, we finally made a connection. She loved me. Needed me. And I was there for her. It was the best time in my life. But then she met Alan. He took her away from me. She grieved less. Went out more. Then they got engaged. She asked me to take their wedding photos. I'd been dabbling in photography even at fifteen. Once she met Alan, I was once again on the back burner."

"I'm sorry." No child should feel unloved and unwanted. And no child should only feel love when a parent was in dire straits emotionally.

"I don't care." Chastity laid her phone on the table but kept the gun in her hand. Sissy wiggled and tried to free herself but the ropes were too tight. "But Alan had an accident a week before their wedding. And guess who Mom turned to for love again? Me. We watched movies and made popcorn. We went to photography classes. I had my mom again. Until she met Dave."

Sissy didn't need Chastity to explain. She knew Chastity murdered those men.

"Mom died about six years ago."

Which triggered her to hunt for new victims. Because she'd kindled a need to see women grieve over the men they loved. Her hate for her mother and her love had driven her to a twisted desire to kill. That need had led her to murder James Beardon, Don Breckin and Richard Buxton as well as Kiefer and Todd.

"You privately trained their rescue dogs." Off any books so it couldn't be traced through a paper or digital trail. "They trusted you. It's why they let you inside their homes." Another thought struck her. "Did Brad even want Abe to call me before?"

Chastity smiled, revealing her answer. "My house had a water leak and Brad offered to go see about it. While he was gone, I told Abe that Brad wanted him to call and check on you."

Did she know Coco was awake? She dare not mention it.

"You know," she said, "my only comfort as a child was my dog. I got a job at a shelter when I was only fourteen. Dogs love unconditionally. They don't wait until they're lonely to shower you with affection. Dogs always want to be with you. You matter to them. They never move on to someone else or something else."

Unlike her mother, Sissy reasoned. Her mother's love had been conditional, or at the very least selfish.

"I would have never moved on from Todd had he not been murdered. When someone dies, we grieve but we have to keep living. I know I'll see Todd again because he knew the Lord."

"Oh, don't give me that God and heaven stuff. When your time is done, you're done. There's no afterlife, Sissy. Hate to break it to you."

Chastity had no living hope. She enjoyed tearing couples apart and watching women grieve and die in agony and hopelessness. Sissy understood it all now. She drew in a breath and let it out slowly. "You can show me the videos of Todd. I'll bear it because I know I'll see him again." Probably sooner rather than later. "You can't take my hope. You can take my life. You can make me sad for a moment. But I know Todd is at peace and I'll be at peace. And you will not be able to capture that last grief shot of me—which is what you want. Isn't it? That's what you were doing with Coco. Making her watch Kiefer's death. You did it with the other women too, didn't you?" Chelsey and Vera believed that was the case based on Coco's circumstance, and she needed to keep Chastity talking. More talking meant less killing.

Chastity's eyes narrowed to slits. "You better believe I did. Just like with my own mother. It was epic," she hissed.

Like a junkie with heroin, Chastity had been chasing the feeling of seeing her mother's ultimate grief, believing she deserved it for the pain she caused her. She continued killing when she couldn't experience the full effect because these women she'd targeted weren't her mother.

"It won't be epic this time. I'm not playing your sick game."

Chastity lifted her chin. "If you know you're going to see him again, then why have you been on autopilot and mourning this long? How was that living?"

A deranged killer was now speaking truth.

Sissy hadn't lived. She'd checked out of life. Todd would have scolded her for it too. "You're right. I wasn't. I guess I didn't care so much about the fact I'd one day see him again and focused on the fact he wasn't here now. My child who would have been part of him wasn't here either and I sank into depression. I stayed there." But God had been faithful to her and never stopped showing His kindness or His goodness.

Now it was too late, because by the time Beau found her, she'd be dead. She'd have no chance to admit she loved him and wanted a future with him.

"Until Beau Brighton entered the picture. Admit it. You've moved on. Betrayed Todd like my mom betrayed me."

"No. No, I haven't betrayed him. I've done what he would have wanted. Loved him always— as I do—and also moved forward to find happiness again. You can't take that from me either."

Chastity snarled and then smiled. "We'll see. Let's watch a video together."

Beau had been kicking himself for the past two hours for not staying with Sissy at the facility. He'd been terrified when he saw the blood spilling from underneath the storage closet door. Once he'd broken in, he'd discovered the body of the senior trainer for the facility. Brad was nowhere to be found, but the police had a warrant and had found photos in the crawl space of his home. He'd been right under their noses. In Sissy's family's home even. Abe must have interrupted Brad with Sissy and he'd killed him.

So many photos. They told a story. One of Sissy's loss and grief. Clearly she wasn't only recently targeted for interrupting Brad's attempt to murder Coco, but she'd been a target for far longer. And her husband's death wasn't a tragic accident but a murder. One that, according to Rhode, Sissy wasn't supposed to be involved in. Joining Todd in the car had been a last-minute decision.

Dom had put out a BOLO for Brad Fordham. But that wasn't enough. Rhode, Stone and Bridge were all using what resources they had to find her and trying not to panic. They'd already lost one sister.

At least Stone hadn't blamed him for this one. But he felt responsible. However, he was not running away or throwing in the towel. Now he was on his way to the support group in Austin with a photo of the dog training staff that included Brad. He'd lifted it off the wall in the entryway of the training facility. Eleanor, who ran the group, had seen a man with the murdered women on more than one occasion and Beau was certain that man was Brad. He parked on the same street by the coffee shop and darted to the other side, then hurried into the church. He found Eleanor in her office.

She startled at his entry.

"I'm sorry to barge in, but the woman with me last time is missing. Is this the man you saw with Babs Arlington and hugging Edie DuPont?"

She studied the photo. "Could be, but it was far away and I'm not certain. But I definitely know her." She pointed to the woman who worked the front desk, the one who'd eyed him when he'd gone to pick up Sissy at the training facility.

"How do you know her?"

"She was a friend of Babs. The one I told you I usually saw after meetings. Real sweet girl. A photographer maybe? She had a camera around her neck often."

Chastity.

All along they'd been looking for a man of small stature. Now he wanted to face-palm his brow. "Do you know anything else about her?"

An older man with graying hair and hunched shoulders entered the room. "Oh, I apologize, Eleanor. I didn't realize you had an appointment."

"Oh, that's okay, Pastor Charlie. This is Beau Brighton. He's a private investigator."

Beau was slightly surprised she hadn't mentioned his connection to the Brighton family and found that he was far prouder of this role. This introduction.

"I see." He shook Beau's hand. "Nice to meet you. What are you investigating?"

Beau sped through his investigation. Time was ticking.

"Have you seen this woman before? Do you know anything about her?"

"Oh, sure. That's Chastity Drendwood. She's Jerry Johns's niece. He owns the funeral home next door. I see her there often."

So that was the connection. Now Beau knew for sure who was behind all the killings. "That's a big help. Thank you."

"We're praying you find her," Pastor Charlie said.

"I appreciate that." Beau rushed outside and next door to the funeral home. Had Jerry Johns known about his niece's sick games? Was he trying to protect her? Hide her? It had been Chastity who had seen them at the funeral home, probably followed them inside. No one would question her appearance there, nor suspect her of anything. She would have known where the casket room was and that the coffins were airtight, so if Beau hadn't found Sissy in time, she'd be dead. It would have ruined the way Chastity wanted to kill her, but clearly she was furious and desperate.

His heart clenched as he imagined Sissy in the deranged woman's clutches.

He met Mr. Johns around the corner from a viewing room. He held up the photo. "You have a chance to redeem yourself, Johns. Where is Chastity?"

Mr. Johns, dressed in another impeccable but thrifty suit, frowned. "I don't know what you're talking about or why you're showing me a photo of my sister's kid. What is going on?"

"Chastity killed nine people that we know of, and attempted to kill another woman and has abducted the woman who was with me last time—who was locked in one of your caskets. Have you been protecting her?"

Mr. Johns's mouth dropped open. "I haven't. I promise. I had no idea. You said you were looking for a man."

"Well, we got that part wrong. What can you tell me about her?"

He frowned. "Well, to be honest, Chastity always had a weird fascination with death after her father died. Her mom worked, so she came here a lot and sat in most of the services, though I told her she could stay in the back. She said she liked them. It was strange, but I simply thought it was a way to process her own father's death."

Beau wasn't sure if he believed Mr. Johns or not. "Did you know she was here the day Sissy was almost killed?"

He nodded. "She'd come by for brunch. We'd just gotten back. I had no reason to suspect her."

She must have seen them come inside and thought of it as a prime opportunity—or hoped for one.

"I am telling you I had no part," Mr. Johns said. "I'll help in any way I can."

"Where would she be now?" She wasn't at the training facility, but Sissy had mentioned before that she and Chastity were the only part-time workers. "A place she might go to be alone." Surely she knew they'd discover Abe's body, look at Brad—whom she'd also framed—and then when that went south they'd hunt for her. Could she have killed Sissy and gone on the run already? He banished that thought as quickly as it entered his mind. He simply couldn't fathom Sissy not being alive. Not being part of his life. He'd never stop until he found her.

Mr. Johns rubbed his chin with his forefinger and thumb. "Well, her dad had a cabin near McKinney Falls State Park. She liked to go fishing with him there. But she said she sold it about six years ago."

When the first murders began. "I need that address." Beau surmised Chastity hadn't sold that cabin but she didn't want her uncle to go out there. She wanted it private and secluded. But for what? To develop the photos? Would they find a wall covered in images of death and grief and pain?

"Sure. Let me get the exact address. I need to call my wife." Beau followed him to the office, taking no chances in case he'd been lying and was tipping off Chastity. But he called his wife—

he heard a woman's voice on the other line—and then wrote down the address for Beau.

He took the paper Mr. Johns held out. "If she calls you or contacts you in any way, please call me immediately."

"I will. I definitely will."

Beau raced to the truck and hopped in, putting the address into the GPS and starting the route. "Siri, call Rhode."

The phone rang through his Bluetooth speakers and Rhode answered. "Whaddaya got?"

"An address to a cabin. And, Rhode, it's not Brad. It's Chastity." He gave Rhode the address. "It's about twenty minutes away."

"We'll meet you there. Do not go in unless there's imminent danger. Wait on us. I'm calling my brothers and Dom now."

"I won't go in, but if I see she's in danger… I'm not waiting. I love her, man."

Rhode sighed. "I've known that since you were fourteen. It's the main reason I gave you lead on this case and left you to it. I knew I just needed to get the two of you together for more than five seconds. Duh." He ended the call and Beau pressed the gas down.

Sissy had to be alive.

Sissy had been working the thin ropes tying her to the chair. She'd just endured one of the hardest things ever, watching her own husband's murder. Chastity hadn't lied. In the same fashion as Kiefer's murder, Chastity wore a camera, like a GoPro, knocked out a dazed Sissy, then suffocated Todd with the airbag after he'd begged her not to harm Sissy, who was pregnant with their first child.

He'd been a brave hero to the bitter end.

Sissy had forced herself to watch without flinching. Without giving Chastity what she wanted—a complete come-apart. There'd be no final photo. No candid to remember her most shocking moment. She'd made sure to ruin that too.

Now there was nothing left to do but die. She needed more time. The ropes were loosening. She just…needed…more time.

"What is this place? I never knew you had a cabin."

Chastity peered out the window as if awaiting someone. Sissy was hoping her brothers and Beau would put it together. They had resources and would stop at nothing.

"It belonged to my dad. He took me up here sometimes to fish for the weekend. Mom never came, though. Never a fan of the outdoors."

"Chastity, where are my dogs?"

"Enough with the dogs!" She grabbed the gun off the table and stomped upstairs. Sissy took the opportunity to work furiously at the ropes. Chastity's backpack was in reach and she knew she kept hiking gear in there, including a Swiss Army knife.

She rocked in the chair until it turned over, and then she drew the bag to her and unzipped it. Sweat ran down her temples and her heart beat wildly, but she found the knife. She opened it and went to work on sawing through the thin rope.

Footsteps upstairs kept her on edge. She didn't have a lot of time.

Finally the ropes were hacked enough for her hands to break free. Then she worked to cut her feet loose. She rushed, her fingers fumbling. Then finally the rope snapped and she jumped up and headed for the door.

That was when she heard footsteps on the stairs to the second level.

Not just Chastity's. But little scratchy feet.

Lady and Louie.

Sissy's dogs were here! She grabbed a lamp off the table and raced to the wall connecting with the stairs, keeping her back flush against the wall and waiting.

She was getting her dogs and fleeing this nightmare.

Beau crouched in the woods, surveying the cabin, but the blinds were drawn and it was quiet inside. Chastity's car was parked out front, so she was definitely inside. Beau's insides jackhammered and he wanted to rush in, but it could get

Sissy killed. He couldn't think that she might already be gone. His brain wouldn't let him go there. Neither would his heart.

He'd parked about half a mile back and hiked to the secluded cabin. The rest of the crew was coming from Cedar Springs, so they had a longer drive. If only he could be certain of Sissy's safety inside.

The minutes ticked by and then he heard a noise in the bushes and spotted Rhode, his brothers and Dom making their way to him. "Any line of sight?" Stone asked.

"No," Beau whispered. "Can't hear anything either. I don't know if that's good or bad."

Bridge inhaled deeply. "Me and Dom are going to take the back. Rhode, you and Beau keep to the bushes in case it goes sideways, and, Stone… you see if you can get in the front door."

Stone looked at Beau and smirked. "Beau, you back me up. Rhode can cover the perimeter. You did good work finding this place."

Beau bit down on the emotion caused by Stone's approval. Stone had been tough on him but maybe Beau had taken it wrong because of the hard hat his dad had always been. "You sure?"

"I reckon you love our sister as much as any of us, so you'll do everything to make sure she lives and gets out safely."

"Does everyone know how I feel?"

They all nodded and gave him don't-be-an-idiot looks.

"Okay, then."

They fanned out to their designated positions, and when they were in place, Stone looked at Beau. "You stay at the porch steps while I try the door. I'll give you a nod if it's unlocked. Then we enter and you can stay behind me. I have no idea what kind of weapons this certifiable woman has, if any. We tread lightly. If anything goes south with me, you don't worry about that. You get Sissy and get her to safety. That's all I care about. You understand?"

Beau nodded, his adrenaline racing. "I understand."

"Then let's go save our girl." Stone made his move, going at a stealthy, silent pace. Beau kept his weapon in position. He squatted at the porch steps as Stone paused, listened and tiptoed up the wooden stairs to the front door. He cocked an ear, then carefully put his hand on the knob and twisted.

Turning back, he nodded once at Beau.

The door was unlocked.

Beau crept up the stairs, then put his back to the wall opposite Stone.

That was when he heard the bloodcurdling scream from inside.

FOURTEEN

Sissy whacked Chastity upside the head with the lamp when she reached the last stair. She howled and staggered, giving Sissy the chance she needed. The dogs came running and jumped on her.

"Come on, babies. Come with Mama." She raced for the back door because it was closer, the dogs on her heels, but as she neared it, Chastity tackled her. She cried out as her head hit the floor.

The front door swung open, slamming against the wall. Chastity yanked Sissy from the ground, her arm around her neck and gun at her temple as Stone raced to the kitchen, then froze.

"Hold up," Stone said calmly. "Put the gun down. It's over."

"It's not over," Chastity hollered. "It's never over."

Sissy tried to remain steady and still, but she couldn't stop shivering.

"Let her go."

"How about I let her grieve." Chastity moved at lightning speed and turned the gun toward Stone, firing.

Stone collapsed on the tile floor.

Sissy gasped. Chastity turned the gun on her. "Oh, that look... That's priceless, Sissy. I only wish I'd have had my camera. Now you can go to Todd in all that peace you talk a good game about."

"She's not leaving this earth yet. Put the gun down." Beau stood with his gun trained on Chastity.

Chastity snatched Sissy by the hair, dragging her in front of her body like a shield, only part of her face peeking over Sissy's shoulder.

"Oh well, this is fun." Chastity laughed. "The rich boy attempting to save a woman who can't get over her husband. Which one of you will grieve the other most? I want to see that." She pressed the muzzle into Sissy's temple and Sissy tried not to whimper.

"You don't drop that weapon, the only thing you're going to see is your grave." Beau's gaze was steely and his jaw set, his hand steady.

He and Chastity were locked into a standstill until Beau glanced at Sissy. "You trust me, darlin'?"

Sissy whispered, "Yes. I trust you. I trust you with my life."

Gunfire erupted, sending a ringing through her ears.

Chastity dropped to the floor, and Sissy looked up, stunned. Beau had made a shot that was near impossible.

Beau raced to her. "You hurt? Did I graze you?"

"No." But she'd felt the heat of the bullet whizzing near her cheek.

The back door splintered and cracked, sending Sissy into another spasm of screams, and Beau readied his gun, but it was Bridge. He'd kicked down the door.

"Stone's been hit!" Beau said.

Bridge called 911.

Rhode and Dom entered the house. Bridge checked Chastity's pulse more out of habit from being in the FBI than believing she'd survived a gunshot wound to the head. The blood turned Sissy's stomach. "She's dead." He looked at Beau. "You didn't have a lot of skin to work with. You could have hit Sissy." He grinned. "Nice aim, man. Nice aim."

Sissy's fur babies joyfully attacked her with kisses. She knelt and loved on them and cradled them to her. "I missed you." They looked to be in great shape. Chastity might not have cared about human life, but she'd cared for her dogs. For that, at least, Sissy was grateful.

"Sissy, are you sure you're not hurt?" Beau

asked and stepped over Chastity and the pool of blood forming around her head. He kicked the gun away and squatted beside Sissy.

"I'm okay." Tears started running down her face. She couldn't control them anymore. "She killed Todd."

Beau sat beside her and pulled her to his chest. She laid her head against him and the dogs squirmed and crawled over the both of them. "I'm so sorry."

"How did you find this place? I thought it was all over for me."

Beau kissed the top of her head. "You really think I was going to let the woman I love die in a cabin in the woods?"

He loved her. She hadn't heard him say those words in ages and the honesty and depth of sincerity this time overwhelmed her, sent her heart into a stutter and tears into her eyes. She'd believed him then, though his actions hadn't backed up his words. But now...now she had no doubt he meant them, and he'd proved it countless times in these past days. "I guess we have a lot to talk about."

"You better believe it."

An ambulance and cops showed up, taking away Stone on a backboard and Chastity in a body bag. Sissy gave her statement and Bridge and Dom handled the police. Finally, they were free to go. After her brothers hugged her nine thousand times, they trekked down the road to their vehicles and Beau and Sissy followed behind. The next few hours were a whirlwind. But Stone was going to be okay.

The media had smothered them. Beau had gone from just a few short months ago being a prime suspect in a multiple murder investigation to now a hero. But he'd stated the real hero was Sissy. Her cool head and bravery had saved her life.

He drove her to the ranch with her dogs, who continued to stay on her feet.

"So now what?" Sissy asked.

"Now you tell me if you love me back. And if you do, we have some planning to do." He grinned and her heart skittered.

"I love you back and I mean it. You're not a mistake."

His grin widened and he drew her into his arms, his lips meeting hers with a tender promise to love her until death did them part. She had no idea how long that time would be, but she would cherish and make the very most of each moment God allowed them to spend together.

Six months later

Beau stood outside the brand-new home that he'd built on a patch of property about three miles west of Sissy's family ranch. The house wasn't grand. A modern farmhouse with two stories and a wraparound porch. A big yard where the dogs could play and hopefully children someday. Farther back on the property was a huge pond and he'd had a pavilion built for family get-togethers. Probably not his family. His father had commended his job at finding Coco's attacker and a serial murderer, but it had come with the words that this job was going to bore him eventually and he'd end up messing it up with Sissy Spencer.

Dad was wrong.

Coco had been released from the hospital two days after Stone went in. She finally remembered all the details. Chastity had been invited in on the pretense of discussing the charity for dogs. She'd worn a black stocking cap, but they now assumed it had been a ski mask rolled up in case she needed to conceal her identity on the way out. She must have pulled it over her face when she'd heard Beau enter.

Sissy and Coco had been working through their trauma together, and with Eleanor, the support group therapist in Austin.

Stone had spent about four days in the hospital and was released.

And Beau had gone into Austin and bought Sissy a two-carat princess-cut diamond ring. Nothing over-the-top because she wouldn't have liked that. He'd driven her to the place they'd spent that summer night they shouldn't have, but the place had always been theirs and it seemed fitting to propose to her there.

She'd said yes to it all.

They were to be married next month, outdoors, with all the fall colors in bloom. The month of thankfulness. And Beau was most thankful for Sissy.

"What are you thinking? I said your name twice," Sissy said and wrapped her arms around his waist from behind, laying her head against his back. "You having second thoughts?"

He released her hold and drew her around where he could see her, embracing her with one arm and brushing her hair behind her ears with the other. "Never. I was thinking how much I love you. How grateful I am for you and thankful to God for giving us a second chance. For forgiving us and having mercy."

"I like those thoughts." She grinned and he kissed her nose.

"You still sure you want to marry me?"

"Never been surer."

He kissed her then, in awe of the fact that this woman chose him. After everything. If ever he'd seen a picture of the goodness of God, it was in this woman.

"But I'm not sure about the Texas longhorn for a groom's cake."

Beau laughed. "Sissy, I don't care if there's a

groom's cake at all. As long as there's a bride and that bride is *you*."

"Well, that you can be sure of, my love."

He did not deserve this woman or a second chance, but he was grateful that God had other plans and he'd spend his life showing her.

* * * * *

*If you enjoyed this
Texas Crime Scene Cleaners story
by Jessica R. Patch, pick up the
previous book in this miniseries:*

Crime Scene Conspiracy

Available now from Love Inspired Suspense!

And be sure to look for
The Garden Girls *by Jessica R. Patch,
a full-length suspense thriller from
Love Inspired Trade,
available May 2024!*

Dear Reader:

Sissy struggled to move forward in a new normal, but there is no timetable on grief or a schedule. But she put her feet on the ground day after day, trusting God and that He still had a plan for her in the after. Beau dealt with shame from his past, but he clung to God for hope that he could change and be seen for the man of faith he'd become. Both had to rely on God for all their strength. Some days were better than others. There is hope for us too, if our hope is in Christ.

I love to hear from readers and connect with them through my newsletter. Sign up and get Patched In at www.jessicarpatch.com.

Warmly,
Jessica